Acknowledgements

Various sources aided my acquaintance with Georg Fridiric Handel and his times, among them H.C. Robbins Landon's classic, *Handel and His World* (Flamingo), Norman Lebrecht's jovial *Hush! Handel's in a Passion* (Andre Deutsch), Richard Luckett's *Handel's Messiah – a Celebration* (Harcourt Brace), Philip D. Morehead's *Dictionary of Music* (Bloomsbury), and Donald Jay Grout and Claude V. Palisca's famed *A History of Western Music* (Dent), *Aristocrats* by Stella Tillyard (Vintage), the indispensible *The Penguin Dictionary of Quotations* (Claremont) as well as numerous delightful recordings of Handel's work and attendance at concerts. I have made no terribly serious attempt to rehearse the events of the composer's life accurately or in chronological order. None of my sources is responsible for my fictions or my errors.

F.J., Galway, August 2000

There is another and a better world.

Kotzebue: *The Stranger, Act 1, Scn 1.*

Was there ever a girl more prickly than Atalanta?

Ovid: *The Art of Love, Bk Two*

Writers constitute a universal secret order, a freemasonry, a Grand Lodge of stupidity.

Claudio Magris: *Danube*

Overture

The door opened. My father came in. He found me sprawled across the bed, my books under me, on the floor, everywhere. 'You've been up here a long time,' he said. I felt embarrassed for him. He thought I was masturbating. I was not. I was creating a language to go with the country I'd created, its history and geography.

My window was open and the evening sun streamed in like hot liquid gold over my face, the backs of my hands, over the books with their hesitating pages. My father looked over my shoulder and saw, to my horror, the bits and pieces of my new language, culled from the Latin and Greek I learned at school. 'That's not your homework,' he said. He puckered his forehead. I didn't know what to say.

Then he saw the outlines of the maps I'd drawn, the country with the strange name, the rivers with strange names, the place where I lived, though I could not share that with him. He lifted up a notebook, a handwritten account of the past two hundred years in the history of this fictitious country. He read a page. He tossed it back on the bed.

'It's not healthy to live inside your head like that,' my father said. He left the room, leaving me to the pure sunlight of that most precious of summers, and my notebooks. Fearing that he was right, being older, and that I was in danger of going insane, I tore out the pages of my notebooks and burned them later that evening.

The world I had created did not go up in smoke but curled up my nostrils and entered my soul, where it lives even now.

Fred Johnston is one of Ireland's leading writers. His published works include the highly-acclaimed *Keeping the Night Watch*, along with six collections of poetry. Born in Belfast, he later lived in Dublin before moving to Galway.

NOTE: The townland of Ardreagh and its inhabitants are fictitious. Swift had a living in Antrim and it is said that he visited Belfast. Here he noticed the appearance of a sleeping face on Belfast's Cave Hill which overlooks the city. From this figure, the story goes, he acquired the inspiration for Lemuel Gulliver.

Atalanta

Fred Johnston

The Collins Press

Published in 2000 by
The Collins Press,
West Link Park,
Doughcloyne,
Wilton,
Cork

British Library Cataloguing in Publication data.

Printed in Ireland by ColourBooks.

Typesetting by Red Barn Publishing

ISBN: 1-898256-92-6

One

It was rumoured that one of the McKinley ancestors had gone to America and become President. It was a schoolyard rumour and no one in the grown-up world seemed to have heard it.

I was seventeen years old. It was a time of feeling the chin for hair, gratuitous masturbating, falling more deeply in love than ever again and being hurt more terribly. There was a desperate need to seize life by the throat, strangle it, squeeze it dry of every drop of energy and vitality, to own it utterly. It was a time to own everything and to dream of what might yet be owned. There was great chivalry and great honour.

I was passionately in love with Agnes Fielding, who would have absolutely nothing to do with me but who definitely went into a green pup-tent with Walter Smith on a regular basis. I loved her, as I was to love many women, through the medium of my imagination.

I wrote a play in which she was motif and heroine, and I wrote it in a fair imitation of the language and style of

Shakespeare, with whom we had more or less come to reasonable grips in the final months of that school term. The nights of poring over schoolbooks were done; university was on my father's lips all the time. The results of examinations would come out just after the heat of summer had died down, when a sleepiness invaded everywhere. My black cap and blazer – *Quid tibi opus est?* – were hung up now for good. Come what may, university or no university, I would never slip my arms into those lined sleeves again.

The result of closeting myself in my room was the play devoted to Agnes, handwritten, many foolscap pages in length, every line soaked with love for her. My mother and father muttered of their boy going to university and I had created a world in which Agnes and I lived, exhausted from the effort of battle; and I had no doubt in my mind which world I preferred. Her blonde hair and denimed legs killed me. She called me names and pointed out, constantly, the wire brace on my front teeth. She teased me and treated me abominably and I loved her more. And everyone else teased me about what Walter Smith and Agnes got up to in the pup-tent, the rattling edge of which I could see over the fields at the back of our house.

The tent was like a floundering green pea in a soup of waving yellow. Now and then there was the risk of a blast of salt-pellets in the legs from a farmer if you were caught in the wheat. And beyond the fields were the sea and fishing boats and my uncles and one or two cousins straining at the nets.

In front of our house were more fields, more houses, the steeple of the village church, a marsh, the lough with its watch-tower – sentinel there since the days when smugglers roamed here. To the north, behind thick groves of trees, you could make out the gaunt Georgian manse the McKinleys lived in.

And in the first week of my freedom, my grammar school days over forever and the world at my door and Agnes immortalised, Mr Reginald McKinley passed away.

Two

The McKinleys had once owned, it was said, a papermill in Belfast and at least part of the old rope-works. At their poorest, they were rich. They were gentry and seldom let anyone forget it. They employed Catholic below-stairs staff, which was the fashionable thing to do. There were doting old maids in our village who had seen service with them and could remember old Granda McKinley shoving them aside with the heel of his shoe if they were polishing the entrance-hall when visitors came.

Two sons had died in the First War, a third in the Second. One or two more had gone away, left the peninsula never to be heard from again. Crows had gathered in the eaves of the great house. Sad. The McKinleys were dying out, one way or another. The house didn't look so hot these days.

There had always been one window blazing with yellow light – an upstairs window – and sometimes there was the sound of music, old music, from the window. Then even *that* light went out. That was in my father's young day. Eventually a son came back from, it was said, Australia. He was tall, grey-haired, as old maybe as my own father. Suddenly, a few years ago, he decided to marry. It was in the papers.

We all forgot that feudalism was over, for the most part, and decorated the single street of the village with bunting, hanging flags up around the bayonetting statue grandly and inaccurately dubbed the 'Unknown Soldier' – *To The Glorious Fallen of Ulster In The Great War* – in the square. The woman he married was very much younger than he was. Now he was dead and she was still alive; a very pretty woman, by all accounts, in her thirties. No one knew where she came from and it was even said she came from Australia, having followed McKinley from there. These stories are not meant to be believed. But I saw her at his funeral and she was very elegant, mysterious, steeped in black and veiled.

Over the church a slightly frayed Union Jack clapped in a reluctant, salty breeze. The stiff pews were crowded and it was stifling hot. The coloured glass in the long, ancient windows seemed to creak and strain. Light hummed against the brass plates along the walls: Donated by the Family and Friends of Esther McAuley – *The Lord Giveth and Taketh Away*; In Loving Memory of my Husband, the Rev. Joseph Thomson – *And in My Flesh Shall I see God*; To the Loved Memory of Maud, Our Daughter, Drown'd Feb. XXI, 1831 – *Suff'reth the Little Childr'n To Come Unto Me*; In Memory of Richard and William Fielding, the 23rd Company of Foot, Killed in Action at Ranjapur, July 18th 1842 – *The Lord is My Shepherd*; Donated by Arthur McKinley Esq, In Loving Memory of His Wife Josephine – *Behold I Shall Tell You a Mystery*. This last one intrigued me. It still does.

White gown immaculate in the stale churchy light, Reverend McAspey led the service. The coffin with McKinley in it sat quietly on its bier and didn't move. Sunlight splintered itself in a thousand colours on the worn stone flags of the aisle. Fresh flowers of all colours had been vased and preened. An infant's cry was stifled. Somewhere, a door slammed. My shoes creaked and my neck was stiff. A burst of profane laughter sneaked in through the half-open church doors from the funeral attendants outside, you could hear their feet restless on the gravel.

We prayed for the soul of Reginald McKinley and later the electric organ burst into the opening bars of Bach's *Tag und Nacht ist dien, du machest* . . . which was beautiful and stirring and no one knew the words, even in English. Reverend McAspey referred to the deceased as '*our brother in Christ*' and reeled off a restrained sermon on Joseph in Egypt, then announced a hymn, number and title. Everyone rose, throwing up draughts of sweaty air. Throats were cleared. A tired brownwood eagle stared in mid-flight, Reverend McAspey's enormous bible opened over the stretch of its waxed wings. His refined, treacle-thick voice boomed outrageously over our heads. The organist struck some wrong notes very loudly. We were all embarrassed to have to look at our dog-eared hymnals; some didn't bother, and mimed. The combined breaths of the congregation rose in a heavy sudden stench, as if we had uttered blasphemies. There was a very old man a few pews away whose narrow spotted head twitched violently every few seconds; he couldn't help it, and on either side of him people tried not to look.

I found myself standing up at one point on the outside of the pew, my hymnal in my hand. I was tired now and edgy, the air was getting warmer and thinner and it was hard to breathe. The invisible child cried more insistently. And I looked up and caught Mrs McKinley's eyes staring down at me.

She was standing at the end of a pew, as I was, and had turned the upper half of her body to look down the aisle. Her veil was lifted and she had the most wonderful, most terrified eyes I had ever seen. My father had often hypnotised a ferret in the headlights of our car at night. I had that same kind of fear, mesmerised, beyond reach. She looked at me and looked away and the singing – God knows what the hymn was now – went on and on like an out-board motor – *drone-drone* – and I caught myself on the edge of slipping away into sleep.

It was the greatest summer of all time. We carried Reginald McKinley out of the neat, tended churchyard, past all those eloquent, leaning tombstones, beneath the feeding sycamores, through the rusting wrought-iron gates. Up, then, along the melting tarmac road, between hedges over which sleep-eyed cattle peered with callous disinterest, past my house, my father's egg van parked at the side, up past Agnes Fielding's house and then Walter Smith's house and through the village and beyond, where work had already begun on a housing estate.

We stopped outside the gate of the McKinley house and the coffin was shoved gently into the back of the hearse: *Dust Thou Art* . . . Then Mrs McKinley and one or two others got into the cars behind the hearse and off the whole thing went, back again, to the churchyard, where McKinley was buried in the family vault; great shifting aside of stone, scraping of iron bars and locks. McKinley was lodged away and it was all over.

I began that very afternoon, I think, to understand that all did not last forever, nor was Man immortal. And the sound of that grinding stone door folding over on McKinley filled me with a desperate need to believe in some sort of God.

What if I were to look for Him, and He wasn't there?

Three

My father had wanted to be a fisherman. My mother had been afraid of his going to sea. For as long as I could remember he ran an egg delivery van around the peninsula.

When he had any time at all he'd take me with him down to the quays. Here, drowning in salt and fish smells, we'd sit and chat aimlessly to one or two of my father's brothers. You could look out through the mist and see the Mull of Kintyre on a good day. How many cran, what the water was like, fair weather or foul: this was the nature of my father's wondering at the world. As I got older, he'd boast about me to my uncles and any other men on the quayside, while he'd take big eyefuls of looks into the boats.

'This wee man'll be going to university,' he'd tell the world.

He needed it to happen, of course. Leaving the sea had to be worth something. They'd humour him.

'He's no goat's toe, your lad.'

I was the reason for everything and the motive for his world having changed its shape. I was his son, his only child. Perhaps through me wider worlds might be explored?

At any rate, he'd boast about me, and I'd smile, feel hungry, not want to be there. By the time I was seventeen the trips with my father to the quayside had stopped. I was pimple-plagued, braces across my teeth, was in heat most of the time and in love only with Agnes and the world magicked me away at the slightest whim into some unexplored land which my father could never visit.

For a time, a month or two, I'd helped him on the van. But that stopped too. He sensed us moving apart and he did not want to interfere with so natural a process. He stood back, as it were, and allowed it to happen with as much grace as he could manage.

My mother, on the other hand, fretted. She saw a terrible day coming when I would no longer be her son, but the property of something or someone else, even myself. Belfast would finish me, she said once: 'The university'll be the end of my son.' This was said over a quiet, otherwise uneventful tea, shortly after my seventeenth birthday.

My father, I remember, looked at her, seeing in her face and perhaps hearing in her voice a hurt he had not known before. 'That's foolish, woman,' he said. He brought the curtain down on her. Clearly he did not understand, and he could not console her. She was already ill by that time and neither of us, of course, realised it. She was beginning to feel the onset of that creeping terror which, in the end, devoured her, left her weeping in an iron-smelling hospital bed until her heart gave out.

But that evening at the tea-table there reigned, for what seemed like an eternity, a dust-filled silence in which no words could live. A spurt of anxiety crossed my belly.

What was I afraid of?

Four

Sometimes I would find Agnes walking up the road on her own. Even from a distance I knew it was her. I'd buckle with fear and apprehension. Would she slag me for the braces on my teeth, or the fact that I was skinny? What would come next?

Agnes was small, blonde, always wore denim jeans and had a round and beautiful face. My head filled up like a balloon when I thought, with great pride and a magical feeling of wonder at my own imagination and its power, that I had transfixed her for all time to the pages of my great tragedy. Alone, she saw me and her head went down, from embarrassment or similar anxieties to those which I felt I did not dare to guess.

The sun blazed through the wheat like the suns of Van Gogh in the prints tacked on our Art Class wall. A breeze, smelling of salt, came up from the sea. Trees muttered and you could hear the engine of a car or the sound of a motorcycle miles away.

Agnes would come up to me – unable, really, to avoid me – and plunge her hands into her pockets, straining the fabric across her most delicious and, to me at any rate, forbidden parts. In these awkward, eye-shifting, foot-shuffling moments the game of sexual politics grew serious; there were moves to be made, key words to drop, certain tilts of the head and curves of the mouth for emphasis or pout. Everything was deadly serious.

Agnes may well have been meeting me on an open road in broad daylight not a mile from the village square. But for me, these meetings were on a battlefield littered with unfortunate soldiers who had fought for either her cause or mine, pennants fluttered in the hedgerows and everything was conducted with great honour and a breathless sense of harmony. Nothing was or ever could be wrong, even with my pain, which was part of and served to heighten the beauty of what was happening to Agnes, me, the world.

Her hair, cut short and boyish round her pale face and very large blue eyes, made her look like old advertisements I'd seen for soap.

'I found these,' she said. From one of her tight pockets she produced two tiny sepia-toned photographs. She handed them to me. 'Over by the McKinley house,' she said, 'down their road. Aren't they lovely?'

I turned them over in my fingers; anything touched by Agnes had a special quality, a sort of holy significance. The ancient photographs were glued reverently on to cards which proclaimed: *Abernethy, Photographers, Belfast*, and left it at that as if there were no more to be said and the people in the photographs were not important. A boy, dressed in sailor suit and stockings; a little girl, wide-faced, standing beside him, in white frock and with her hair in curls framing her face. And on the other photograph, the image of a man, seated, with a great and carefully-manicured moustache, severe Victorian frown; behind him, a woman with a thin, pulled-in waist, long fanning skirt, high collar at the throat with a cameo brooch; and behind them both the painted canvas backdrop, something vaguely pastoral for a severe commercial family.

The hard facial expressions unsettled me. Were these two the parents of the little boy and girl in the other picture? *Could they be?* There was something cold and dreadful about the photographs. They seemed to have been plucked out of an album of unmentionable horrors, the kind common to all families. It did not seem right that they should have been unearthed by Agnes. They belonged – I recalled McKinley's funeral – in the tomb. More than anything else, the photographs filled me with a delicious and paralysing revulsion for the past, when photographs spoke the damning truth.

Behind the photographs there seemed to lurk a bottomless darkness; I could not have imagined either of those adults laughing or kissing each other. And this struck me as horrible beyond belief. There was something almost blasphemous about these photographs in the hands of Agnes.

'And this,' Agnes said.

Before I could react she'd planted a soggy parcel of tissue paper in my hands on top of the two photographs. Then she turned, let go her great devastating laugh, and trotted off up the road again, out of my day, off the battlefield.

I had a fair idea of what was wrapped up in the tissue, I could feel the rubbery rim; so I dropped it, along with the photographs, which swayed lazily down to the warm tarmacadam surface of the road with a brazen contempt for what I wanted or did not want from life.

The evidence that Agnes was not true to me lay on the road and did not move.

Five

It was a hot, vicious night, and I woke up with the notes of a piano in my ears. They still half-belonged to dream.

I lay in the grey dark of my bedroom and watched the shadows on the wallpaper. Familiar shapes, frames of photographs, a Jimi Hendrix poster. Against the wall leaned a cheap guitar. I was listening to Bob Dylan records and trying to play along. A pile of second-hand paperbacks in a corner. I had discovered Steinbeck, Erskine Caldwell, William Faulkner, writers very different from those we'd had drummed into us in school.

All that was over now, of course. I could choose my own books.

The shadows on the wall did not move and through my window the fields shone with a light coating of silver frost. There was no moon, but the sky was clear, dark blue, studded with stars. I could hear a breath of wind hiss in the trees. I lay on my back and let my fingers stroll between my legs.

And the notes of the piano sounded again.

We had a piano in the living-room. With relatives and friends, we'd gather round it at Christmas and sing hymns and old family songs and drink strong steamy punch. It was very old and out of tune. Now and then I tried to play it, but it was my mother's instrument. These days she'd lost interest in playing it. There were sheets of music on top of it, photographs of my father standing beside a Morris Minor; standing with an arm around my mother's waist; standing with his brothers in thick-knitted pullovers on the quayside. Two brass candlesticks, shaped like an 'S' and made, it was said, in the shipyard in Belfast, stood guard at each end of the piano.

The notes of music were soft, formal, steady. I did not want to open the living-room door. When I did, the notes ceased abruptly.

A broad slab of light lay over the furniture, the floor, filtering in through the curtains from the stars. The lid of the piano was closed. When I tried to open it I found it locked, as I'd expected.

I stood in the darkness of the living-room and felt, not fear, but a delicate sense of peacefulness, of contentment. It rose up from somewhere uncanny within me and flooded through my blood with a shiver.

Leaning self-consciously against the piano, I felt that there was nothing in the whole world that could make me afraid again. I consigned the notes of the piano to the realm of dream and lazed contentedly in a waking dream of Agnes and me being married in a field decked with coloured tents, surrounded by knights and ladies: this had all taken place in my play, so there was no reason why it should not take place in real life. And I was being married to Agnes with great pomp and ceremony, when my filmy gaze happened to shift to the floor. I had to put my head at an angle to see them properly.
The photographs.
Lying beside the foot-pedals, near enough to them. Although I knew they were still back on the road where they'd settled

when I dropped them. Along with Agnes' other token. But no. There they were. The children, the stiff couple.

I bent down, picked them up, looked at them in the thin light and felt my inviolable happiness melt away. Again I was aware of pain, from somewhere behind the photographs, somewhere just out of sight. And with an awareness of pain came fear. I ran back to my bedroom, forgetting the photographs, which I probably dropped again. I got into bed and heard the springs creak in my parents' bed next door, a reassuring sound. I did not sleep much that night. In the morning the photographs had disappeared.

That next morning the fields wore a faint but undeniable shadow, as if something had passed over them, and I had no appetite for breakfast. I said nothing about my nocturnal adventurings with pianos and photographs. My father believed my imagination was unhealthy and my mother fretted over me anyway. Sometimes I felt as if I were a burden to them, I was on their mind so much. I drank my tea and ate some Hovis bread and longed desperately for Agnes. But she seemed farther away then than ever before. My play, my dreams, my hopes were all sham and emptiness. There was sadness and anguish even in sunlight. I locked myself away in the bathroom and tried to masturbate, concentrating hard on girls I'd seen, on Agnes, although she was sacred. What I wanted to do with those other girls I would not dare to do with Agnes. My sense of nobility and honour was over-developed. Perhaps I knew this: I knew Walter Smith. At any rate, I could not masturbate with any degree of success and fumbled my trousers up and washed my face and returned to the world.

My father was standing by the open back door reading the headlines of a morning newspaper. As I passed him I saw at the corner of my eye a large front page photograph of what looked like a human body, covered in a sheet, half on and half off the pavement. My father sensed my eyes. 'Some things they shouldn't print on paper,' he said. 'Bad enough these things happen, but we've to look at them with our breakfast.'

Photographs again. How much pain they concealed! I scurried into the yard, sending our half-dozen scrawny chickens dashing madly about their wire pen, throwing up protesting cackles that seemed to shatter the glassy air of early morning. Still some frost on the fields, and the hard merciless yellow sunlight, and seagulls gliding over the trees like flapping silk scarves.

Six

There wasn't much to do, but doing nothing carried a heavy, delicious quality. The village square: the shadow of the Unknown Soldier and the way the light foraged in the green metal folds of his uniform; the sound of the bus from Belfast coughing through; the newspapers dumped in a soft thud outside M'Whinney's front door; dogs asleep and twitching under the ancient shadow of the dried-up horse trough; old men in tweed caps leaning on walking-sticks and negotiating the distance between Ernest May's public house and the bookie's office just in time for the start of the English races; always there were Agnes and the unspeakable Walter Smith.

Small, wiry, a great footballer, Smithy had the dark-eyed, dark-skinned complexion peculiar to small fishing villages where foreign boats, at one time or another, have, so to speak, put in. I nursed this peevish notion of his *otherness* deep in the untidy closets of my mind every time I saw him. I'd be leaning against the wall of M'Whinney's, eyeing the books, the newspapers, half dead for want of the outside world in this my seventeenth year. Up would come Smithy – a ferret, the small animal who'd hang on by the teeth and worry you to death. A smile, irritatingly, on his face, the face of one who has conquered. An innocent opening: 'What are you doing here?' 'Nothing,' was always my parry. I would wait for his next move. He'd look around, scanning the square, perhaps looking for Agnes. Well, she'd come to him, that was the story. But not in my play, she didn't. Smithy was hacked to death by a broadsword in my play.

'When are you going to get them teeth straightened out, Bugs Bunny? Your mouth is like a barbed-wire fence when you talk.' 'That's why I don't open it too often, not like some.' 'Are you trying to be smart?' 'Don't have to try, I *am* smart.' 'You're useless, you big willick. More meat on a crutch and your head stuck in books and your hand on your dick.' 'Thanks very much, Walter, I'm glad to know you know so much about me.' 'I'll stick that wire mesh thing down your throat if you try to get smart with me.' '*Thank you, Walter.*'

I had this exasperating habit of trying to intellectualise against the threat of physical violence. It has its drawbacks. Smithy was a physical animal, he did not think things through, he worked on pure emotion. There are people like that. Talking to them, trying to argue a point, is madness, because they have neither the control nor the patience to argue back and, I suspect, they are afraid of words.

This time he drew off, retreated, mainly I suppose because of my proximity to M'Whinney's front door and Smithy's father was a regular customer. Smithy was a bully and I was his foil; suitable enough as one, because I rather enjoyed teasing him. I felt vaguely superior, with my bag of words. 'You're too damned smart for your own good, wire-head,' Smithy said. 'And Agnes Fielding wouldn't pee on you if you were on fire.'

With this my demon departed, walking bow-legged – I took this as further proof of his inferiority as a human being – across the square, under the Soldier's bayonet but not close enough to it. The holy sun blazed down on him and me, locked in an age-old battle. I looked after him until the figure of the widow McKinley passed between us.

I had not, in church, noticed how thin she was. She walked with infinite patience, or slowness, as if weighed down by something. She was like one of those curious long-legged waders that pick the sand with their needle-beaks. She wore a wide-brimmed hat that was a kind of error on her head, and a dress that swam and flowed luxuriously around her thin legs. No jacket, just this flowery, bright dress that seemed unbecoming to a woman whose husband had recently passed away. Even I felt that she was over-dressed and I wasn't one to hold with convention. She carried a bright red bag, square-shaped and bright and hard as blood to look at. One hand held the brim of her enormous hat down against the light breeze of the square and she appeared to notice no one and nothing as she progressed at right-angles to Smithy's retreat.

Watching her aloof passage across the square intoxicated me. There was something in the infinite delicacy – the out-of-this-worldness – of her walk. She had, it seemed to me, stepped from one plane of existence on to another and quite unsuitable one. On this lower level, life had condemned her to move and breathe like the rest of us. I stared towards her face, sought the eyes that had locked on mine that day in the church. Her head turned slowly, like the head on a mechanical doll, and those bright star-points burned through me. She did not stop walking, did not remove her hand from the brim of her hat. But she held my gaze and there was, unless I was very much mistaken, the faintest hint of a smile on her thin, almost invisible lips. Her pale face belonged on a cameo brooch. I looked into her eyes and felt more uncomfortable than ever before in my life.

Suddenly, she stumbled.

The spell was broken. Her foot seemed to turn inwards, or get caught in something, and for an instant she staggered, or seemed to, and the whole picture went out of focus. When I looked again the widow McKinley had her back to me as if I did not exist and never had existed, and she was moving out of sight behind the statue, in her own world. Her sudden drop from aesthetic grace had shocked me, as if a church spire had suddenly collapsed on a congregation; perhaps now I would say it was as if a wrong note had been played in the middle of a quiet Chopin study. The rest of the day seemed to reverberate with the explosion of discord. The world had been tilted off its axis. Behind me, the voice of old M'Whinney muttered darkly, 'A quare woman to dress like thon, and her man not cold.'

Despite the presence of the sun, I shivered as I walked home. I found my father sitting alone, 'Your mother's not well, son. The doctor's been. She may have to go into hospital.'

My mother was lying in bed, over the covers, apparently sedated. She spoke in low whispers. 'I'll be all right, son. It's just a woman's thing. See that your father's not worrying.' But I went outside and found my father sobbing quietly to himself where he thought no one could see him, in the front seat of his egg van.

There was so much darkness in my world, and there was no one to whom I could confide my own feelings, those which had not been demanded by the moment, by someone else's sickness or sorrow. I had looked upon the face of the widow McKinley and found her to be beautiful, and there was no one I could tell. And the feelings her smile had wrought in me were utterly beyond my experience.

And with all this, I was alone.

Seven

My father had a place of darkness inside him and in these days he showed it to me. Sullen, morbid, terrifying, he could not get out of it. It was a windowless, airless locked room, around which he paced through his days, unaware of the passing of time – and of me.

Eventually, I was making his breakfast and watching while he refused to finish it and at night I lay away far in my own world listening to his distant sobbing, that virtually interminable agony of mind and heart that my mother's illness and absence had brought upon him. He could not shrug it off, and he did not drink. The harbour became a place of mourning; the pilgrim in him had gone away. Once again I was reminded of the lamentable fragility of life. Perhaps tomorrow I too would be mourned.

I counted for very little; the anguish of this thought drove me farther beyond the borders of my created world. I was writing things almost every day now: stories, poems, not very well crafted, outlines of dreams, fantasies, efforts at description.

My play to Agnes seemed at times, when I thought about it, to have no substance, however much it granted me some relief from the intrusion of the world; I did not know that the child was beginning to inspect the creatures of his imagination more and more as a man. I wrote almost in proportion to the increase in my father's sorrow. When we would drive to visit my mother in the hospital in Belfast it was, for me, like visiting someone I had once known but was beginning to have difficulty recognising or communicating with. Flat-haired, grey-faced, trying to prop herself up on a pillow was not the affectionate and irritating mother I had known. Everything this theatrical image did was for effect; to show there was no pain, no illness, no despair, no terror, that all was as it should be, that the iron-and-sweat smells of the bed were the dank flowers amongst which her soul lay content.

Neither my father nor myself was fooled. The visits forced him into silences and tears and groans. I grew to resent them. They made me think of demands other than those which my imagination laid upon me. I could not appeal to anyone, I was alone. Alone with my guilt and increasing selfishness. Home again, I would crawl sheepishly out of my father's well of sadness and into the brighter light of my bedroom and my imaginings. I regretted having destroyed my new language, new country, new people with their new history. I resented the man who had made me destroy them. That man, of course, was my father. We learned to live in each other's uneasy shadow.

During the days I walked the country roads alone, no longer wishing to meet Agnes or anyone else, for that matter. I allowed the sun to daze me.

One day Agnes walked past me, noticed I didn't bother to say anything, and promptly followed me. 'Have I done something on you?' she asked. 'No,' I replied. 'Well, I thought I had, the way you walked past me.'

I looked at her, at the face I had loved so much, and saw it, probably, for the first time, as beautiful but flawed. I could not then appreciate that her beauty owed everything to the flaw. I saw only, very briefly, that Agnes Fielding had dirt in the corner of her eyes and that this was the ugliest thing I had ever seen. 'Well, that's the way', I said, and walked off stiffly.

I did not look back, although I wanted to. No: that was over, that gasping, mad part of it. Besides, I owned Agnes every time I wrote her name on a piece of paper or dedicated a poem to her. She would never have understood that and the thought might even have scared her a bit. Perhaps it was on that particular day, proud of having begun to conquer myself, as I thought, that I walked until I found myself outside the wrought-iron, paint-peeling gates of the McKinley manse, the long, black, gravel drive running away between enormous trees that dripped leaves, light coming in dry hard shafts through the branches and a welcoming silence drifting down that drive that was as invigorating as a breath of sea air in my face.

Eight

There I was, then, standing between the stone gateposts, looking. An avenue of trees, sunlight through their branches, a sense of wonder and mystery. Behind me was the grey world, with its distractions, demands and disappointments. I had been a failure there. Nothing had charmed me other than Agnes, and I had begun to lose faith in all that. She could not come up to the majesty of the figure I had created in my play about her.

My father's increasing remoteness suited me. Newspapers and broadcast media bore news of an even broader world than ours in which new terror and murder held hands. But it all might as well have been taking place on the moon. This avenue of trees, with its shafts of light like blades quivering and slicing back and forth, was more immediate and therefore more real. The great black, wrought-iron gates hung back on their rusty hinges like broken skeletal wings. Two stone globes topped the pillars of the gates – I went in.

Fear is an odd thing. At seventeen it drifted round behind me like a pup and nipped at my heels. I could not confront it, for when I would turn around, it was gone. I could smell the hot tarmac under my feet and feel the stroke of the sun on my face when a sliver of sunlight fell there. Without looking around again, I knew that the gates were beginning to disappear behind me, the world from which I'd come slowly beginning to dissolve into thin air.

On either side of the drive broad green pasture-land rolled off for a long way. Behind the raucous tumult of birds I sensed a deep and impenetrable silence. Briefly I was carried back to Rider Haggard novels; I was not yet aware of the greater and more ordinary adventures. I walked on, unaware of the distance.

Now and then something lively scampered in the tough undergrowth beneath the trees. But it was the height and solemnity of the trees themselves which caught my breath. I would bend my neck back and stare up at them and see the sun winking away up there and wonder how many years of growth surrounded me and what secrets they contained. Now there was no other world but the green-brown one through which I moved; now nothing else existed but myself and the trees and this drive – there was not enough room for anything else.

At the end of the drive there was another gateway, this time its architecture imitated a miniature castle, with two turrets for gateposts. Two worn elephants roosted on their tops. Ivy crept all over them. Despite the heat, there was an oppressive heavy dampness here.

I did not want to pass through this gate but felt oddly obliged to do so. Suddenly the McKinley house reared up in front of me. It was now about a hundred yards away. No dogs; I'd listened very carefully for the sound of dogs. I did not know how many people from our wee village had ever been up here. Not many, I'd suppose.

The house was covered in creepers and ivy of various colours. It was smaller than I'd expected and not at all frightening or sinister. A convenient country house, four-storeyed; a big gleaming door with a shiny brass knocker in the shape of a heart; curtained windows with frames that came almost all the way down to the ground. Two tall, precarious chimneys and confident red brick beneath the beard of creepers and ivy. Behind it, blazing like a burning mirror, a lake. I had never been told of a lake up here. But then, who'd tell me? I stood looking at the house and trying to figure out what it was disturbed me about it. A voyage from one world to another had been made – of that I was very sure – and there was no way of knowing what to expect. I looked at the big windows with their drab, unmoving white curtains and noticed, squinting my eyes to see better, that paint was flaking off the immense white door. I felt the weight of the McKinley house, of its age, its weariness. I had never seen a house dying before.

Then there was the music.

I did not so much hear it as merely become aware of it, as you might become aware of someone standing beside you.

It drifted down from one of the big windows, crackling away as the record turned on an old machine; but the voice was sweet and the notes pure, even to my adolescent ear. And I seemed to have heard some of these notes before, but I could not recall where or when.

The music was quite wonderful, gentle, Italian opera, but I could recognise nothing else and besides that was about the limit of my classical music education. The sadness of the sound of that music against the backdrop of the lake, the tired old house, and the sun dripping over everything like melting butter; I had felt just such a sadness when, thinking of Agnes, I had written milky words into her mouth as a character in my poor play. Anguish that was no longer endurable, that had to cry out, spilled down from the crackling record player. I stood and listened and wanted to scream out my own longing, my own emptiness, that the silence in which I lived my daily life suffocated me.

'Beautiful, isn't it?'

I turned, then, knowing who it was. Mrs McKinley. Standing between me and the old world forever.

She moved with an animal's instinctive grace, between the

marble fireplace and the curtained window. When she moved into the light I could see through her dress, her legs, their watery lightness, and I felt distinctly uncomfortable.

She placed me in an enormous cushioned chair and I sipped tea from a delicate china cup which had figures of archers on horseback pursuing a stag painted around it. I could revolve the cup in my hands and watch the hunt. Tall, surly potted plants stood by the fireplace like servants in ridiculous fancy dress. There were thick carpets, portraits of cross-looking people staring down from the walls, a piano whose wood was polished to a mirror-sharpness, and frail-looking windows which opened out on a garden at the back of the house and gave a comforting view of the lake with the sun on it. Birds bantered loudly in the garden trees.

She was standing by the long front window now, dressed like a young girl going to church, everything about her made of water and air, fragile as the cup in my hand, ready to disintegrate. I could not take my eyes from her, her hair now down around her shoulders, her face softer and paler than I'd noticed it before, no sign of widowhood about her, her frame full of restrained life. Now and then she went to the enormous darkwood dresser behind the piano and lifted a decanter of golden-coloured whiskey and poured some into her teacup.

When she had invited me in, a mixture of fear and anticipation had flooded me. Now that I was here I knew that she had taken the key to whoever I'd once been and tossed it into the depths of her sparkling private lake.

The ancient record-player hummed and squeaked near the flung-wide garden windows.

'Handel,' she said from her place by the curtains. 'I love Handel. Have you any interest in music?'

I sipped my tea. 'Indian,' she said, watching me.

The room was gloomy in spite of the light breeze blowing through it from the garden and the scent of dying roses which, I noticed, seemed to follow her about.

'No,' I replied, I had not much interest in classical music.

But I told her I had heard the tune before, the tune which had just finished.

She turned to me, her face as pale as chalk. 'When was that?'

'I think some time when I was a child,' I said.

The memory of the piano playing in the dark of our sitting-room, the memory also of the old photographs seemed out of place here. Again the hint of roses as she turned. I saw that she was even younger than I had imagined, And her *accent*. Slight, hard to place, loosening some of her vowels, tightening others. I sat with my knees together in the chair, drifting in the breeze-thick bluish gloom of the place. I raised my eyes and saw a dusty chandelier swing limply above my head. The whitewashed ceiling was dull with time and dust. There was wallpaper of a type, ornate yet delicate and hopelessly faded. Pictures, too, perhaps, screened in shadow? I imagined weighty conversations in this room, their terrible importances melting into the walls. When she had pushed open the big front door I had been afraid of the vastness of the hallway, the winding staircase going upwards into unimaginable silences and rooms with sealed doors.

Inside, the house seemed bigger than it had appeared from the drive. At times, seated in the luxurious chair, the room seemed to throb or vibrate with a passionate unnameable loneliness, so that, warmed by the Indian tea, I felt chilled by a sadness similar to that which had once overtaken me only when I'd curled up in my bed and thought of Agnes. All that was unattainable in the world seemed to be gathered up in that room. It reeked of mourning, of loss. Dreams dried up here, fell away like petals off a dying flower.

She turned from the curtains and moved – almost as if her feet did not touch the carpet – across the room towards me. I stared at her and felt my eyes widen. She smiled, a girl's smile, the creases around her eyes barely noticeable. Suddenly she stopped in the middle of the room and glared into her teacup; the teacup now dishonoured with whiskey. 'Do you know who that was singing?'

'No,' I said.

'Well, that was my mother,' she said. 'She was a great singer, perhaps one of the greatest. She made recordings, that's one of them. In her youth men committed suicide for her.'

Wonderful, then, the sweep of her arms as she set the cup and its attendant saucer on the mantle over the fireplace. Brass candlesticks adorned here, unpolished, dull in the dull light of the room. The roses, crushed by some violent upheaval of the spirit, spun their perfume around her once again. Her body disturbed me. It made me feel guilty in a way that had never happened to me before, even in those heartsick moments when the heat of masturbation began to subside. My throat was dry, my hands had begun to sweat. I put my own cup on its saucer on the massive arms of the chair, terrified that it should topple over.

Roses and whiskey, blended together with something far more powerful and deadly; the sweet animal odour of her body. I had never encountered anything like it. It frightened me, aroused me. I felt that, were I to stand up right now, I would die of embarrassment, my discomfort pushing against my trousers. My heart beat a steady rhythmic tattoo beneath my shirt. I wished she would go away, that the room would go away. But everything remained just where it was.

'Committed suicide,' she said. She smiled. 'Can you imagine such a thing? Because they wanted her and she would not have them. Because they wanted to imprison her and she was too free for them. Have you someone who would commit suicide for *you*?'

She turned her eyes on me, stared at me, her smile dissolved now, the room broken and cold. I grinned nervously.

'No,' I replied, 'I have no one who would kill herself for me.'

'Then you must find someone,' she said.

She took me through that enormous remote hallway and opened the big front door.

'You must come again. You must promise me you'll come again. There must be no going back on your word.'

I promised. My heart could not do otherwise. She smiled at me, her eyes penetrating, sad. Then she added an absurd formality by holding out her hand for a handshake.

'My name is Atalanta,' she said, 'after Handel's little opera. That's what you heard on the record-player. I play it every now and then to remind myself of who I really am.'

I took her hand, the cold fragile flesh. There was no grip in her fingers, only in her eyes. I turned my back on her and knew she watched me as I walked, trying not to run, down the driveway and towards a life which was no longer mine, in which I had become a disinterested spectator.

Nine

My father stared at the television when the news came on. He seemed to take it personally now, the sporadic irritating acts of violence. To me, they were happening in another world. There were our trips to Belfast to see my mother; her legs had swollen hideously now and she lay bathed in terror in a private room. Then there was the slow, patient accumulating stench of rotting, which I didn't mention to my father, who behaved as if it wasn't there, tucking bedclothes around my mother, kissing her forehead, reassuring her, cracking silly jokes that broke my heart to hear. He would grab a doctor in the polished silent hallway and demand explanations for this, descriptions of that, holding his sleeve as a drowning man clings to a chunk of wood. He had lost weight and drove his wee van with difficulty, his instincts telling him it would change nothing to keep up a routine.

I understood that, in his effort to keep my mother alive and in his world, I had little part. His suffering, which had grown to include even what he watched on the television news, was exclusive and personal. Selfish too, I suppose, as all grief is. I was left to my own world for most of the time, sneaking into his only to make sure he was still alive there.

Occasionally, neighbours visited, or one of his squat fisherman brothers, and then they'd sit in the heat of the evening in our small front garden and talk about the way things used to be, avoiding the obvious topic as any good sailor would avoid a hidden rock, sailing around it on a current of harmless things. Over their bobbing heads, duck would sweep up out of the marsh, snapping and clapping in triangular flocks.

While they sat in the garden, I would stare out of my bedroom window across the fields towards the sea and wonder by what excuse I might get out of their presence and take off on voyagings of my own up towards the McKinley place. I had not needed excuses to leave the house before; but since everything had become secretive and vague, I had begun to feel slightly furtive and criminal about even the thought of the old house, the music of Handel, the lovely tired grace of the widow who was not a widow but a trapped and dilapidated girl in need of company and, so I imagined, rescue. The days of Agnes had receded very far back into my unique emotional history. Something very new and infinitely more enticing had shown itself.

The chattering of the men in the garden broke over the hot sunny evening like confetti. In the kitchen the radio was playing something brassy and reminiscent of old dance halls. I went down and drank some buttermilk and buttered a triangle of potato bread. I was chewing it, letting the dusty floury heavy slice fill up my mouth, and in the background in the front garden the men laughed at something. Suddenly I felt indescribably sorry for my father and for the whole world.

The sweet bread fouled in my mouth, my appetite stifled. A sadness grew up in me from somewhere left of my heart and threatened to choke me. I knew in that moment that the world contained this sadness to an infinitely greater degree than any human being could feel, but that now and then we were darkly privileged to partake of it. Images from my childhood mingled and merged as I stood, heartstricken, in the kitchen, with the brassy music blaring all around me; my father and mother picnicking like children, giggling, sorting out the sandwiches, the tea, the cake and making a mess of it on a flung carpet at the edge of the old World War Two airbase, the hangars of corrugated iron now rusted and fallen in, grass cracking up between the concrete on the runway.

'I mind the time your uncle Tommy who's in England now and me looked up and saw German fighters and British fighters chasing up and down and round and round and the noise of them. Then there was the night they bombed Belfast. A bomb fell on St Anne's Cathedral there and they haven't finished repairing it yet. I courted your mother in the black-out, no lights allowed in the streets, you know. So you couldn't see what you were getting.'

And my mother would dig him in the ribs. He loved her. That was the saddest thing of all. She would die anyway, despite his love. But I imagined big bombers like the ones they had in *The Lion* and *The Tiger*, taking off from this runway, for Germany, hammering Hitler. I looked and saw them, props thundering and spinning, the smell of petroleum, the smart attitudes of the officers and men as they marched out to get onboard, confident, untouchable. In those days, I would often fall asleep in the car on the way home.

I looked up and it was old Mr Black, at one time the postman, long retired, an officer in the Navy during that very war. He was looking down at me, asking me if I was all right.

'Aye,' I said, 'I'm fine.'

'It's allowed to cry, son,' Mr Black said. 'Do you want to come out and join us old boys nattering about the oul' times? Maybe you'd be better off, than sitting here broodin'.'

'No, Mr Black,' I said. 'I'll go out for a dander and freshen up.'

'Aye, you do that, son.'

'Don't say anything to my Da,' I said.

'I won't,' Mr Black said, and shuffled off to use the toilet.

I'd found the excuse, fully ratified, to leave the house, and I did. The warm air dried my tears. I began walking in the only direction I seemed to know. I knew as I walked that I had cried mostly for myself, scared now that I knew I was part of the human race and as lonely and vulnerable as the rest of them.

Ten

My mother's bony hand clawed weakly over the blankets, her mouth was dry and her thin tongue swept it continuously. Now and then she cleared her throat and tried to speak. So much time had gone by, and so quickly.

Long ago she had ceased being my mother, a busy and fretful woman about the house and a good neighbour; she had become someone else in a distant country and we spoke to each other across great distances when we spoke at all. Her eyes vague slits, she'd see me and try to smile. The effort of watching her caused me intolerable embarrassment. Yet it seemed to be my duty to sit there in the darkened room and attend her. Her voice was cracked and parched as burnt wood. And there was the thick presence of an odour of rotting, animal and hot, which stayed in my nostrils long after I'd left the room.

My father, meanwhile, would try yet again to salvage a doctor from the wreckage of coming and going in the shiny corridors, to obtain arcane and vital information about his wife. He was seldom lucky, yet the exercise seemed to do him some good in that it kept him away from the dark and hideous room in which my mother dissolved. Her pain came, it seemed, in short but knifing spasms, and she would call out my father's name and try to prop herself up on one useless arm, her face contorted, the painkiller wearing off too rapidly, more rapidly each time, scaring her with its impotence.

Like something wounded by a shot from a hidden thicket, my mother would glance quickly around the room as if to track down the source of her pain, then fall back against an enormous dented pillow with my father's name on her dry lips like a magic formula which produced phantoms but nothing more substantial. My father would come into the room, no doubt expecting her to have died while he hunted in the corridors. She would close her eyes as he propped the pillow up behind her, the agitation in his voice scarcely disguisable. How could she distract him from the desperate business of forgetting her?

As my father fumbled about the bed, my thoughts fled treacherously homewards, to a gate, a driveway, and a house where light shone in a window, and the music of Handel, whoever he was, broke over a gleaming lake like a breath. In that utterly different place I had left something of myself. Its call was merciless and strong. Now and then I would slip over to the window and stare out at the damp courtyard and over it and a wall topped by barbed wire to a compound crammed with purring impatient green-painted armoured cars, their aerials whipping and vibrating in the rainy squalls. Two worlds, always. And it was so often a matter of choice. I longed to be back in Atalanta's front room, the lake behind us through the open doors, her magical body leaning this way and that, my own body aching wonderfully. Again there would be the photographs and the scent, the old record-player and the music, the mystery of the closing away of the rest of the world. I needed it.

I stared out at the armoured cars and then walked back to the bed in which my mother's breathing had by now been rendered rhythmical and artificial with additional painkillers, and I knew deeply that I had been right to invent, to unstopper my imagination, to creep inside myself, to forsake the harsh-edged daft pain of this world for the creative and deliciously dangerous world of my own secret vision.

Nothing was more terrible than the embarrassment and pain suffered by my father, the helplessness of my mother, and the ominous toyland playfulness of armoured cars. I could not construct the shapes of these out of plastic model kits and some glue. They did not come in a cardboard box for two shillings and sixpence, paints extra. No. Neither did they come from a manoeuvrable world of imagination. They were not controllable.

There was so much that was not controllable in the world and it terrified me. Impatient to get away, I would fever about the room while my father consoled my now-unconscious mother and kissed her forehead and settled the bedclothes for the hundredth time, a ritual made all the more distinct by its futility. Then we'd be in the van again, wipers on, coloured lights and neon signs distorting through the wet windscreen and fantasising all over the inside of the vehicle, empty egg crates rattling and clashing in the back and the odour of chicken shit and eggs and petrol clotting everything.

The mix of vapours and the motion of the vehicle often made me feel sick. I'd stare out, dazed, into the streets of a city rendered magical and constantly changing in the rain and reflected lights. Figures mingled and dissolved into each other along the pavements. The buildings reached up tall and endless like great dark fingers into a faintly throbbing greyish sky, and now and then the firefly light of a helicopter would dance across the rooftops with its drumming song. Soldiers would step from the back of Land Rovers with a tender slowness that resembled a ballet, their first steps on to solid ground melting in the rain so that, for an instant, they seemed to walk on black air. At a checkpoint their young painted faces looked ludicrous, even comic, as they moved from window to window, peering in, ritualists and players in some incredibly well-rehearsed epic drama in which even my father and I had been granted parts. Everywhere, though I doubted whether anyone but myself could hear it, there hung a soft music behind the curtains of rain, a music devised by dark and remote angels whose eyes were mirrors of murders committed in back streets and whose fingers plucked the triggers of illegal guns. It was they who blew gently on the corners of streets and flicked the ragged pages of newspapers into the air. It was their fingernails which pricked static across the radios of soldiers and policemen at windy roadblocks and in freezing doorways. Somewhere along the road home I would fall softly into sleep dreaming things I could never remember.

Eleven

A moth, red-winged and frantic, fought to live in the folds of light white curtains.

Beyond the window Atalanta moved along the edges of the lake, the sun shivering on the surface of the lake like liquid fire, her hair hanging carelessly, but with immense fragility, on her shoulders. Today she dressed in light blue slacks, a blouse of sorts. She seemed to invite informality, now that I had wished myself into her company and she had, somehow, accepted me. I was there, a nervous awkward presence, behind the curtains, not spying on her, spectating more than anything else, in her world but hardly part of it. In my fidgety hands I adjusted a cup and saucer, sipping tea which she had offered me almost before I'd been framed in the massive square of the front door.

Being there was trimmed with an impersonal magic. I could no more stay away, now that she had introduced me to the utter loneliness of her world, than I could stop myself from breathing, She was everything my impoverished heart lacked: mystery, promise, the half-missed heart-beat, the dry mouth of longing and anguish. She had given me tea, offered me also the depths of the armchairs, and turned away through the windows into the garden and down to the lake. The house seemed to hum, a single barely audible note. I felt uncomfortable, alone in that bright room. I imagined myself watched, observed, and the various odds and ends, trophies of other lives, the piano, seemed curiously alive. I walked out through the open windows and descended slowly, cup and saucer in hand as delicately held as I might hold the open flower of a tulip. *Committed suicide*: the phrase rang like a dark bell in my head. Her mother had caused men to die by their own hand. There was something desperately romantic and appealing about the notion. But behind it, as behind a child's story-book cartoon, the message was blacker and terrifying.

Atalanta stopped, turned, saw me approaching and smiled. Now was I naked before all the world. Perhaps she had meant me to take my tea and go away quietly, unobtrusively, certainly without further disturbing her. I did not know what to think. I knew only that when she smiled I was unable to think. Today she did not play recordings of her mother's singing and the silence over the lake was immeasurable and plaintive, like some lines of classroom Wordsworth. I had no world worth being in but this.

She held me, drew me towards her, with the smile. The cup and saucer had acquired generous weight, and I looked, gawkily, for a place to put them down. There was nowhere. I felt the daft-looking adolescent I must have looked, the dreadful realisation that I was not as mature or adult or any of these things, as I thought I was. And I was not in control, not here, not in front of her, at any rate.

Suddenly a thin squadron of duck blew out of cover far over the lake and the noise startled me; the cup and saucer, of course, tipped, slanted and curved towards the earth. The whole structure cowped and fell out of my hands as if it had decided to. There were natural balances in the world and I had upset them.

Drowning in embarrassment, I went down on my knees doubled as if I'd been shot and began the humiliating procedure of trying to put right the devastation. It was like trying to remake the world. It could not be done. I felt Atalanta standing near me like a divine judgement. But it was more than that; my manliness had unbalanced with the cup and saucer, the outsplashing brown tea. I could not recover it. I was a boy again, ungainly, stupid, spotted and with at least one bad tooth. The braces seemed to grow in my mouth. I was on my knees before all the lovely and desirable things of life and that, perhaps, was where I was bound to remain.

Then Atalanta was kneeling beside me. 'Here,' she said.

She opened something inside me that enabled me to stand up smartly, recover something of the man I thought I was becoming. In a wink she had righted everything, the cup was back on the saucer, they were both in my hands, the duck had vanished. Had she conjured them up to cause this upset? I was no longer able to think of ordinary things. They were for the bleaker, more troubled place from which I had emerged to this house, this lake, and Atalanta herself. They tried to intrude even as I stood there, a fragmentary illusion; a hospital bed, wringing hands, the smell of melting flesh. No – I would not permit this. I smiled. I smiled at Atalanta and felt my soul turn over like an egg being fried in a pan – *flip!*

'You might have stained the knees of your new jeans,' she said.

The jeans were too blue, too neat, too absolutely perfect. They felt hard and unbreakable against my legs. And they were, it appeared, all Atalanta, widow of Mr McKinley, could see of me. I looked at my feet, at the grass. A light breeze ruffled the tiny hairs at the back of my neck.

'*Faulse beauté qui tant me couste chier, rude en effect, ypocrite soulceur*', she said. 'Do you learn French at school?'

'Yes,' I said, 'of course.'

'François Villon,' Atalanta said, moving slightly uphill, towards the open eye of the French windows, the curtains like albino lashes. 'I hate all beautiful things except music. Music is more than beauty. It is the soul of everything that lives. I don't expect you to understand that. You probably think all pretty things are beautiful and therefore good, don't you?'

The beginnings and end of that accent, curious, unplaceable; I raised my head, wondering if she had mixed tea and whiskey again, before I arrived. She spoke quickly and as if to a larger audience, somewhere just above my head. Did angels stroll restless and invisible in this musical place? I had done five callous years of French and never once heard of François Villon. Certainly what she spoke was odd French, as if it were from another age. It was, of course.

'A thief,' she said, 'a man of the streets, he loved women and wrote about them and got into fights. A pagan, but pure.'

She moved off up the incline of the garden and my eyes fixed stupidly on the curves of her thighs and bottom. I saw, or thought I saw, the elliptical lines of her underwear and felt, ridiculously, crassly, the stirrings of my flesh. The true humanity of Atalanta seemed to lie along those barely discernible outlines. For Villon I had no further care. Yet she talked as she moved up the garden, as if only the angels were a proper class for instruction.

'You think that everything you see is beautiful and therefore good. A man is handsome, therefore good. A woman is beautiful, therefore good. That is the surest road to tragedy. Yet it is one we all take, every time.'

She turned to me now, at the top of the garden. I stood, teacup in hand still, a monument to my own absurd appearance and yet entranced by her, by everything, unable to move, to act independently of her next word or command.

'I will show you the beautiful,' she said. 'Come with me, I will show you the only innocent things in the world.'

Twelve

Villon: I spun the name around, its two sharp syllables, one tight and high, the other nasal, long, in my mouth until it worked on me like a hypnotist's soft voice.

I walked along behind Atalanta in a kind of acolyte's trance, watching the heels of her shoes lift and fall, aware of the lake to one side, the big house diminishing behind us. A faint trace of scent held in the air behind her as she went, tantalising, beyond naming. I thought that if I recited the poet's name long enough something magical might happen. But nothing did, nothing of the cinematic sort. I became aware of the utter uselessness of my midnight scribblings when people such as Atalanta existed. Compared with her, the house, the music and now, the name of the French poet, all in a dancing combination, my imagination's work was nothing. Perhaps, I told myself, Atalanta was more my creation than anything else – had I imagined her turning her head, looking down at me, in the church a hundred years ago? What had happened to lead me to the edge of this lake, this thin, dry path towards the black bulk of trees? I became convinced that I had entered another world where other rules applied. Nothing quite ordinary, or answering to strict ordinary injunctions, could happen here. Atalanta moved everything according to her likes.

I moved, therefore, as she bade me, spurred on by the force of the magic she spun around everything, that incredible warmth of presence. I thought of McKinley, how much older he had been, how she could ever have felt anything for him. Love, I understood, was a thing which came and went with age. I thought too of Agnes and felt very little, as if I had left her on the shores of another and very distant country, a false lover promising nothing and refusing to write until time and circumstance had withered us.

Now the wall of trees, pines mostly, reared over both of us like a scented curtain. Atalanta slipped off the path and vanished into them. Afraid to be alone in front of their weight, I jumped after her. She slipped from shadow to shadow, from shaft of sunlight to shaft of sunlight. Motes of dust, nets of flies, scurried and hovered in the yellow folds of light. There was the stifling smell of pine, and sap ran stickily over my fingers whenever I leaned a hand against the bark of a tree to steady myself. Ahead, Atalanta shuddered and stopped in a circular clearing blazing with white, clean light that had the quality of water. A little low white-washed wall surrounded a patch of earth in which, planted like hideous and ugly fungi, miniature headstones leaned and seemed to nod. Here and there, visible when I leaned over, names, names culled from vague and mildly unappreciative childhoods, from storybooks with big pages and hard covers, from playrooms where sunlight and loneliness kept company.

Atalanta kneeled forward, creasing her knees now in the soft twiggy matting of the circular glade. In her fingers, tiny blue-headed flowers had appeared mysteriously, although perhaps not unexpectedly. Towards a leaning headstone she extended her arm and lay the flowers beneath its soft childish shadow. The name on the headstone – *Tammy* – seemed to sing a little as the flowers jiggered and rearranged themselves in the light tree-filtered breeze.

'They are all here,' Atalanta said, 'the innocent ones. The ones who had no say in the world's sufferings. If we were all like that, what a different place this would be.'

Cats, she explained, and dogs, and even a rabbit; all buried with a grace and sanctity given only to the realm and passions of children.

Generations of McKinley nurseries had enclosed the sounds of weeping. The names, Tammy, Winnie, Arthur, Felix, all came from a time of crinolines and sailor-suits, of family stiffness and parental absences, Bibles and death by consumption, when the McKinleys rode to Belfast to supervise women who died of exhaustion before they were twenty, men who sweated themselves into pleurisy and TB before they'd reached middle-age. I'd done my history well. The great houses had their own song, as did the redbricked Belfast mills. But it was still confined to books. Safely out of the way there.

I looked at the pets' graveyard and it all seemed to come alive – the poverty, the pounding threat of dismissal, the way the McKinleys lived and the way other people lived. 'The dates,' I said. 'My Granny worked in one of your mills. Only getting married saved her life.'

I was angry, felt angry and couldn't say why. It had no direction, a wild struggling rage that had crept upon me quietly, treacherously, threatening everything. This world was false, pampered, clothed in its own superiority for the rest of us to see and worship. It took time to bury dead cats, dead dogs, a twitch-nosed rabbit. There was a world which wasn't like that, I wanted to say. That world smelled of putrefaction – a thick, sweet smell – and spoke the language of radios and static.

She knew none of this, she took time to lay flowers at the grave of a cat, while the world strangled itself diligently, slowly, with infinite patience. It could not be the same thing, to bury a cat and bury a human being; I would not allow it. I was turning from the graveyard now, trying to see the way back through the smothering trees. Atalanta didn't move, didn't follow or guide me. I heard her voice rise to catch my hearing as I stumbled, blinded by God knows what, through the sticky pines.

'He took Tammy in his own two hands and held him in front of my face! He twisted Tammy's head around until I heard his neck snap! He did this because I wanted to go to the cinema! In Belfast, alone, just once!'

I fell out of the trees on to the path and stood there, horrified that any sort of pain had intruded into my special world, this new order which I was busy creating for myself, unknowingly, but nonetheless quite ruthlessly. I need it to be untouched, virginal, as I needed Atalanta to be free from any kind of human hurt. I had no care for what had gone before, how the McKinleys had made their money or what my long-dead Granny had endured as a child. None at all. I was buried in the need to exclude these things and others of the same weight. I was smothering in the quite selfish desire to surround myself with myths, however lightly charged, to blot out the enormous silence of the world at the bottom of the McKinley driveway. I did not want to return there. I looked to Atalanta to rescue me and I did not want reminders of her humanity, she must remain much bigger than life.

I walked, heading upwards around the lake towards the house, chewing the words that had followed me out of the trees. Villon had vanished. A heavier criminality seemed to linger in my head. Atalanta's words were an explanation and a plea for understanding. I had triggered her outburst by mentioning the stirrings of my, admittedly false, social conscience. I had forced her to reveal the disorder behind the plaster order, the chaos behind the polished formalities. I couldn't forgive her for having permitted a view of such ordinary suffering. In any case, I didn't understand it. I understood only my own.

Thirteen

He was part of an earlier time and had been endowed with legend. Now he sat in our kitchen sipping thick, heavily-sugared tea, while my father pottered about aimlessly, always listening, it seemed, for some distant sound. Andrew Bell the clergyman, minister of the church.

Andrew had been a fine cricketer, a decent man with a bat – a village hero. I'd always heard these things, Andrew had been a ghost flitting from room to room in my childhood. Once or twice I'd been driven to watch him play in some polite local tournament; I remembered a tall skinny figure in immaculate whites windmilling down the run towards the poised and tapping batsman. The slow unwinding of the game somehow put me to sleep. I do not recall having founded any great childhood admiration for Andrew, he was just there – a village trophy.

Then he entered the Ministry and shortly became engaged. They married, he was ordained, they vanished into Africa, a place I knew vaguely from Evelyn Waugh. Silence followed.

Somewhere in the midst of the silence Andrew Bell and his wife returned. Ardreagh looked on, puzzled. A sunburnt minister, leaner than they remembered, and his sunburnt wife.

Andrew wore Africa like a mantle for a time; I could recall vaguely his deep burnt-wood facial tan. He took up a quiet posting in the country, surrounded by keepsakes and Africana, and preached the soft, reasonable religion of damnation and repentance, reward and punishment. The heady exultation of Africa died away into Waugh's creeper-laden deeps.

Andrew had trekked over, into the Ulster bushland, to administer a kind of comfort to my father. He did not seem to think I required any, and perhaps he was right. Now and then, over sips at his chocolate-dark tea, he would raise chubby and greying eyebrows over a still-boyish face and ask me daft and unnecessary silence-breakers such as how I was getting on at school. I told him it was over, that university was a possibility, not daring to go into details of what dreams lurked in my own privacies. Of Handel and Atalanta McKinley, greying, wrinkling Andrew Bell heard nothing. He adjusted his dog-collar restlessly against the pourings of the kitchen heat. His fingers were fat now and had black hairs on the backs of them. His wide shoulders stretched the grey of his jacket; married life had long ago plumped his gangly cricketer's frame, filled out what Africa had worn away.

We sat uncomfortable over the formica-topped table. Through the window the sun screamed with hot glee over the straining fields. I longed to be out there, longed for the excuse to get out of the way of Andrew's embarrassed silences and his even more embarrassed questions. We did not know one another; you do not know legends. Great canyons yawned between us: I remembered my geography and imagined, sitting there, the Victoria Falls plunging slowly and with vacant grace into nothing, roaring but going down all the time, and the mindless gap that the image created appalled me. Andrew Bell might be a competent minister, but a lifetime ago he had lost his majesty. I yearned backwards, towards the sticky couple of afternoons when he had turned up that fabulous run down towards the enemy's stumps. The hero sitting at the table shone for an instant with the faded radiance of an old importance.

'Why did you give up cricket?' I asked.

For a moment Andrew behaved as if he hadn't heard me. Then he looked up, startled. He seemed to have been oddly frightened by the question. He gave out his answer with a woodenness which made me think of lines rehearsed over a long period of time.

'God called me to do His work,' Andrew said. He smiled. The smile took effort.

'Why did you leave Africa?' I said. Was I aware, then, that I was tormenting him? Yes, most likely I was, I need to torment someone other than myself. I knew the story, had heard it before, had tried many times to conjure up magical images.

'Africa's very different,' Andrew replied.

His eyes seemed to see Africa just over my right shoulder, about an inch left of the kitchen sink.

'People there behave very differently from us, you know. Gladys found it all a bit too much. The women used to dress up in their best clothes, all sorts of colours, and dance into the church, then dance out again and change their clothes and dance back again, like a fashion-parade. It was not what either of us was used to. All the hand-clapping and dancing. I think we were made for quieter things, eh?'

In spite of myself, I kept seeing him whirling up that run towards the batsman, all power and rhythmically-controlled energy. Nothing quiet about it. You couldn't take your eyes off him.

Andrew Bell was a modest, sincere, affectionate big man. He tried not to look directly at me, he endeavoured to keep things as light-humoured as possible. He gave off an almost sublime air of strength combined with sincerity. Perhaps indeed Africa required louder voices.

As he spoke he played with his fingers, rolling them over like fat cigars. At last he stood up. The room filled with him.

Education and Godliness had not softened his abrupt Ardreagh speech.

'Your father's taking it hard,' he said.

He seemed distracted, as he moved around the table. My attention fixed on the large fingers. Gladys. A name redolent of brass flowerpots, geraniums, blacklead for the fireplace and poppies in Flanders fields. There were places, areas in our family over which time had stopped. Andrew, heir to Livingstone and Burton, in his modest manner, was haunted by the odours of carefully-mown grass and the manly slap of leather on wood thick with linseed oil. Africa had been none of him. I watched him pace the kitchen and knew how novels were born. If he ever sat down to write one, he had all the necessary material. Perhaps Andrew and Gladys were of an age long passed. There was a soft, elegant discipline about him; I could never imagine him shouting. He wore a patient quietness around him constantly, like an invisible shell.

Andrew stopped by the sink, the sun through the window hard as wood.

'I once made cricket-stumps out of two paraffin-oil cans and a bat carved out of a piece of church seating that had peeled off,' he said, staring out of the window, back, perhaps, to Africa, the cricket-fields of the soul. 'I used to spend my idle evenings teaching the local lads how to play. They thought it was a very funny game. I told them everyone played it in my country. Is there such a thing as a holy lie? They were all Christians anyway. The Welsh had gotten to them first. They played rugby almost from birth.'

So *that* was it!

Andrew poured the rest of his tea down the sink, washed it away, cleaned his cup, dried it carefully, set it upside down on the draining-board and wiped his enormous clutching fingers in a towel. I admired him again. Beneath the cloth a cricketer pulsed and steadied himself for the long wonderful run down towards the stumps of life.

'I had a way of gripping the ball, like that, see? So that when you let fly the thing was spinning. When it hit the ground the batsman thought he knew the way it would go, but it would spin in on him, hit either his legs or the stumps.'

New life seemed to flash in him, like a spit of hot fat out of a pan. I stood up, found myself smiling, open-faced, and he was more or less the same way. Something of the younger cricketer, the world-innocent, Africa-less layman, content with the praise of his wee home village on the edge of Ulster, sang up in him. The note quivered in his face, and faded. He slapped me on the shoulder, a man going elegantly grey. I thought of Gladys, hearing for the umpteenth time the cheering of excited but undisciplined cricketers under the sacreligious weight of an African sun. Somewhere in the background, delicate china cups tinkled on a bamboo table.

'Your mother was a very fine woman,' he said, his voice turned formal and sad. Outside, there was the abrupt chatter of birds arguing in the trees. Andrew Bell fidgeted, smiled awkwardly.

'She's not dead yet,' I told him, feeling the comic callousness of the words.

'Anything that's not present sometimes feels as if it's dead,' Andrew Bell said. He left me in the kitchen and went out, black Bible clutched to his side, to administer to my father.

Fourteen

George Fridiric Haendel; he put on the final 'e' to Georg in order to feel more English.

The three names seemed to glow in the stuffy yellow heat of the County Mobile Library.

Once a month the big brown truck gasped into the square and one by one, like mourners, slow-paced and reluctant subscribers with their books humbled themselves towards it. I never used the Mobile Library, preferring to buy the odd cheap book, put my name on it, make it mine and become, in this odd way, a continuation of its plot. Here I was, on a hot blue-and-silver day, in the truck on the square under the shadow of the Unknown Soldier forever advancing inland, gaze fixed on the horizon where no enemy waited for him. I was searching about for a book on the composer, knowing agonisingly little about him, and wretchedly aware of having left Andrew Bell and the Good Book alone with my father in a house where silence was already rotting the chairs and doorways and clamouring at the windows.

Miss McCracken, the librarian in the truck, who sat up front with the driver – who never climbed down out of the cab but read a newspaper and smoked unsociably for the duration of the stop in the square – was not a bad-looking woman, and wore a respectable tweed skirt to the knee, pulled very tight over her behind, a light white blouse which dropped far forward when she bent over, revealing tiny mounds trapped in two flimsy white cups.

Sometimes untidy minds made her bend down to locate books on lower shelves. In the heat and closeness of the inside of the library truck, Miss McCracken smelled of perfume and underarm sweat and did not discomfort me much. Once, when we stood eye-to-eye, I saw that the pupil of one of her eyes was green, the other pale blue, and that down on one side of her neck, partially hidden beneath the white collar of her blouse, a huge blue-and-black mole, almost an inch across, flat and ragged at the edges, clung like some abominable clue to some part of her personality. She was shy, nervous, fussy; and now and then she would put her fingers over the part of her neck where the mole was and her sentences would break off half-way through and hold a pause that was long and sensitive, like a kiss.

'Now mind you bring that book back before or at least *on* the date I've stamped on thon ticket,' Miss McCracken told me. 'Otherwise I'll have to impose a fine. That's the rules. Since when are you fond of Handel?'

'I'm not,' I said. 'My father is. He has piles of his recordings. He has a whole collection of composers and he plays the piano as well.'

Miss McCracken fingered her mole and looked beyond me, out through the door of the library truck, down its steel steps, across the square, searching like the Unknown Soldier for something that was no longer there. I did not care whether she believed my lies. I did not even know why I told them. Suddenly it mattered only that I had a book on Handel and that something had been affirmed between me and Atalanta

McKinley. The book was a talisman, a mystical and sacred key. I wanted to be able to talk to the widow in her own language; now when I thought the word *widow*, it seemed incongruous, out of place, a title awarded to venerable old ladies who were poised near death like great birds at the edge of a cliff – No. Atalanta was not poised like that. She was circling, circling, over my head, passing through me, erasing whole parts of my past, substituting something else. It scared me, this inexplicable process of discovery and unravelling. Miss McCracken, who could know absolutely nothing of this and seemed to know only her mole and the inside of the library truck, had already fussed herself away into a corner and an old withered man in a cloth cap, breathing asthmatically and wearing the arrogant and angry frown of old age, was coming up the three steel steps with infinite care. A mischievous elf. I got out of the way.

I was moving with the care of a clergyman across the square when Agnes came up to me. She seemed to belong to a different, older time, when I was different and older too. Something about her had undergone a subtle and determined change. I did not know what it could be. She smiled at me, an unusually pimply smile. That was it, She had acquired acne. I knew all about that, but I could not be sympathetic. That was for Walter Smith to worry about. But she did not look like Agnes. She looked older, slower, and her pimpled face was fatter.

'Hello, there.'

She was making a great effort to be the same old Agnes, to be light and easy about the world. I had found that most attractive and then not very attractive at all. I felt awkward, stopping to talk. I had nothing to say, certainly nothing I wanted to share with her. How things had changed between us! I felt her lack of power over me, felt the weight of my own distance from her. She was suddenly a small, tragic figure, and no one had written a play for her yet.

'Hello,' I said.

I did not want to be there, talking to her, my thoughts under siege. Already Agnes was between me and something greater.

'I don't see much of you around these days,' she said. Her eyes were big, wetter than usual, and I felt so very little. Perhaps what I felt was merely something different from what I had expected to feel, what God knows I had always felt for her.

But the difference, or the loss, or whatever it was, made me impatient. Her face was mottled and blotched and the acne was taking hold on the neck and her forehead. Her beauty seemed to be dissolving before the onslaught of some vicious plague, something not particularly fatal but no less ugly in its symptoms for all that. She shuffled her feet.

'I haven't seen Walter for a while,' Agnes said.

Behind me, the heavy diesel engine of the library truck coughed and growled and I thought of Miss McCracken, up once again in the hot cab of the vehicle, a cab full of cigarette smoke and bored exchanges, divining omens from her mole. Agnes looked up at me and the hot sun cast a shadow behind her that looked weak and thin on the tarmac.

'I'm going to have a wee ba,' Agnes said. 'What do you think of that?'

I recalled one particular scene in my play where Agnes' beauty causes the hero to dismount from his horse and kiss the earth immediately in front of her feet as she stands in serenity and glory outside her tent. The fool who had written that was dead. *Buried.* The lid of the tomb cemented down forever. His memory was being slowly erased. Soon no one would remember his name. But unreasonably my heart was a dark drum in my chest and my palms were sweaty. There were no words left in my mouth, they had dried up, blown away. I felt my breathing deteriorate. I had to get away from her or I was going to faint. And at the same time I felt nothing inside, where things get felt, nothing at all.

'You look like you've seen a ghost,' Agnes said. 'Anyway, what's so big about having a baby?'

But I had pushed past her, brushing her shoulder with my shoulder, and she turned and looked after me and started to laugh. 'It's not yours anyway, it's not yours anyway!' Something coarse and unnatural saturated her voice. She was someone else, a presence in Agnes' lovely body which had slowly but inexorably corrupted it. I managed to fold into the shade at the side of the square and stop myself from shaking from cold, even in the mad heat of that day. I felt as if something had passed invisibly from Agnes to me and infiltrated my body and was now causing it to quake and shiver as if I had a 'flu.

I was gaining my strength, walking slowly but feeling the blood come back into my head, unable just yet to think of anything but aware of a tension developing between what I wanted to think and what was forcing itself into my head, and I was passing M'Whinney's newsagent's when the book on Handel slipped from my fingers and landed spine-first on the pavement, splaying its pages out like so many waving petals on an underwater flower.

There he was: Handel. A round-faced man in a curly wig – *1685* to *1759*. Son of a barber surgeon, in the days when the red-and-white striped pole meant something more painful than a shave. I picked up the book, inspected it to see if Miss McCracken would have reason to forget her mole the next time the Mobile Library came into the square.

And there *it* was, the kind of thing which, now that I knew Atalanta, was seeming to have both significance and a sinister ordinariness about it. Handel had been born on February 23rd. I was born on *July* 23rd. I stared at the number, lending it perhaps, much more potency than it had and wallowing in the potential of my having the same number in my birthday as the great composer. But it was the sheer ordinariness of the thing that sent me shaking, more gently now. On that date, not so very far away now, I would be eighteen, legally free to do what I wanted with my life. Certainly the number was invested with power, it was the date of my release from whatever it was bound me to my quivering, uneasy self; that seemed to walk with me wherever I went, a feeling of not being entitled to give my opinion on anything but being unable to comfortably suppress the need to. A vague sense of imprisonment. Agnes, my father, my mother, even Atalanta McKinley, seemed to contribute something to the unease, the gentle anguish pulsing under everything I thought and felt. Twenty-three, however, was the number to look out for. After that, even on twenty-four, I felt that I would grow new skin, shed the old one, feel the thrust of my wings for the first time.

I picked up the book, forgetting about Agnes, her problems, my faint-heartedness. Mister M'Whinney was after me with bewildering abruptness.

'You dropped this, son.'

He held up the library ticket, turned over where Miss McCracken had printed my name, she'd stamped the date on the opposite side, the only side I'd seen.

As I took it I made out quite clearly, above my own, the name of Atalanta McKinley.

Fifteen

My father, bent-backed in a glowing field of barley like a figure from a French Impressionist painting; Mr McHugh made us look at the rickety slides and knocked us over the knuckles with the leg of a chair if we got out of hand. 'Look at this, boy – what do you think the painter meant with the sun? Any ideas? No? (rap-rap) No imagination, boy. No *imagination*.'

Well, I had no shortage of imagination but usually thought the artist's intentions too obvious to need my paltry explanation. I had the notion that each person interpreted the work differently, that there could not be any imposed interpretation, it was like everyone having a different, but still valid to them, opinion. Mr McHugh worked from books, was a kind of failed competent painter himself, exhibited in the church hall for jumble sales. What, Mr McHugh, do *you* mean by the sun?

Now here was a painting, steeped in sun, come to life. I sat uncomfortably on a low block wall and sipped buttermilk from a cracked mug and watched my father, talking to himself as he usually did when he thought he was unobserved, inspecting the crop, squinting at the sun, sweating, shirt front open a few buttons, something faintly restored in him by this excursion into the earth. Reverend Andrew Bell might have inspected the same wide field, perhaps, with a view to what it might look like were it a cricket pitch. Or maybe he would have enjoyed being younger again, back on a farm not much bigger than this, where the year turned naturally, without much fuss.

A few yards beyond my father, Natty Grier, a bald ball of a man whose acres these were, rose out of the earth like an Old Testament visitation. He shouted something and my father laughed, fingering Natty's crop. The two men enjoyed each other, moving solemnly between the rows of silvery-green, walking at a pace more suited to contemplation than anguish, putting pain away into the good earth, feeling, perhaps, the earth's heartbeat under their feet. A form of communion.

What mysteries that field held! They seemed to be able to decipher them. The stalks swayed, the wind now and then bristled them, the sun shone, protectingly, reassuringly. Crows danced in the trees and cawed like spoiled kids wanting attention. Gulls wound themselves round and upwards in spirals that seemed, if you thought about it with your eyes, to have an upward shape, like an upside-down cone, a solid yet made of air and feathers. There I was; Handel's step-brother Karl was older by thirty-six years, it was his father's second marriage. Like mine, Handel's father did not much trust using your imagination. He did not want Handel to become a musician. But Handel persisted – must I also persist? – and at nine years old he was taken on by another musician named Zachow.

Was it guilt that made Handel study law for a time at Halle University? I saw him then, his father pacing a wooden-beamed floor, debating his future, stern, worried, too much experience and not enough awe. Handel: what would a full wig look like on him? How long must he wait for this discussion to end? In his blood, imagination flowed along with all the other cells, a huge pulsing cell itself, waiting to flower. Pace, pace; I saw it all quite clearly. A wintry day, somehow, a fire glowing in the grate, and the words *I'm only thinking of your own good* steadying themselves against an onslaught of indifference. And was there an Agnes in Handel's life, then? Or an Atalanta? Later, perhaps. Just then the hot stuffy room was everything and the urge to run away overpowering. Handel, clearing his throat, begged leave to disengage himself and he would study matters more fully, alone. That was how it must have been, the compromise. Outside, the town rattling by uncaringly, oblivious to the choices he did or did not possess. That was how it always was.

My father and Natty Grier, over the fields of barley, disappearing slowly into it as if it swallowed them up – behind me the rattle of a pushbike. I turned and closed the book on Georg Frideric. Closed over the door, his father still in the room, but Handel outside breathing more freely.

The postman, second delivery; Johnny Henderson, known to drink too much, a veteran of some war the Americans had fought in Korea. He'd been living in New York for years and suddenly, not much older than me, he was in Korea fighting Communists. He had a permanent twitch in his face down the left side and was the most interesting man we had in the area. Everyone knew him, he was ideal as the postman. He had come home, a confirmed bachelor, with a little money from his war and the twitch. And the strained American accent.

'Letter for you, kid. Might be important, you're getting older now.'

So as you got older, letters got more important. Johnny had this home-grown information tucked in deep along with his other relics of an American past. Like the rest, it meant nothing. His wisdom, even I knew, had been unable to save him from the war.

He handed me the almost-square grey envelope. No one in the entire world would be writing to me. He stood around for a moment, then turned his back and got on the bicycle and moved off, as if my silence had dismissed him. The handwriting meant nothing to me, and, when I instinctively smelt it, the envelope was faintly scented.

I had read somewhere, though not in any religion class, that the Spanish conquistadores had offered the Inca chieftain Atahualpa a copy of the Bible, saying their God resided within. The chieftain, never having seen a book before, put it to his ear and listened. Nothing. Then he shook it. Nothing. Then he sniffed at it. Then he tried to bite it.

Exasperated, he threw it on the ground, saying that it was obvious that nothing lived within the book. To the conquistadores and their leader, Francisco Pizarro, quite opportunely, the chieftain had committed punishable blasphemy. Dumbfounded, the chieftain stood and watched as the people who kept their silent God in a book massacred his unarmed escort, a foretaste of horrors to come.

I do not know what calamities I expected to befall me as I held the envelope in my hand. But, like Atahualpa, my very first inclination was to sniff at it. I opened the envelope. Within it was a postcard, an ordinary enough commercial thing, with markings for the stamp and address. The picture side displayed a black silhouetted portrait, the kind that was fashionable on cameo brooches and in round or oval frames in the days before photography. It was of a portly-faced man in a thick curled wig which fell to his broad shoulders. Beneath his silhouette, the single name and the dates: *Handel – 1685–1759.*

I ransacked the envelope, turned the card over in my fingers. It had been made and printed in Germany, but no other clue to its origin was visible. I felt an emptiness such as the Inca chieftain might have known in the instant before he tossed the instrument of his destruction to the ground. Fearfully, I returned the card to its envelope and slipped both inside the pages of my book.

In the coolness of the house, the sounds of my father and Natty Grier in conversation as they came out of the fields rang like little bells. They comforted me, as I curled up on the nearest and deepest armchair, unable to act, finding rational thought difficult. I did not have to think hard to know, in the end, who had sent the card. But I did not know why. And this lack of knowledge carried its own weight of chilly helplessness.

Along with it came a certain guilt at having a secret I could not openly share with my father. I had always been taught that secrets had no place in a family, that God knew our hearts anyway, that secrets festered like sores if left unattended. I felt the eyes of some watchful and not very understanding Being bore through me. More than anything else I wanted to get out of the house and go back to Atalanta McKinley to a world where secrets were still possible and nothing dreadful happened to you if you kept them.

Sixteen

Reverend Andrew Bell called to pay his respects to Reverend McAspey and that afternoon my father saw him to his bus, shook hands firmly with God's batsman, then loped off homewards, shoulders stooped. He returned too speedily to a precariously real world, and his re-immersion in it caused him obvious pain.

I sat for a time under the shadow of the Unknown Soldier and looked around the square, recognising everything with a familiarity that hadn't occurred to me before. I was so much a part of everything here, and every brick on that square and the buildings around it seemed to have some claim on me. I was both comforted and unsettled by this realisation. I knew that, in order to see myself apart, as something with rights and sensations of its own, I would have to divorce myself from the friendliness and seductiveness of this familiar place. Even as I began to think like this I was filled with intense and almost unpleasurable excitement. The urgency of the task competed only with the devastating wrench away from the security and comfort and knowledge of certainties which it implied.

Already the world about me was beginning to alter its shape and focus without my having had any part in the process. It took a while, but eventually I began to view Agnes' pregnancy with a dispassionate eye. And I was very glad it had nothing to do with me. I was recognising my inherent selfishness, centred on an instinct for self-preservation I didn't know I possessed. It was this and more, a feeling that Agnes was now a liability. Something about her and her condition threatened the good and wholesome restlessness inside me.

How Walter Smith would handle things, I no longer seemed to care.

There was nothing left of what I had imagined Agnes to be, nothing at all. Something in her face, the last time I had stood before her, had almost begged to be reassured; I was no longer able to reassure her about anything and, when I was honest with myself, I realised that I did not want to make any effort, emotional or otherwise, to save her. She had passed over into a realm of ordinariness and mundanity that did not interest me in the least. She was, truly, a being belonging to another planet, speaking a language of word and gesture to which I had no response.

Other changes were taking place, ferocious little alterations in focus. I was no longer as self-assured, as confident as I had been. Familiar things were trembling, acquiring ghosts which flitted through my memory with unnerving speed – Agnes was no longer Agnes, my mother had become a mysterious and aloof shape in a hospital bed, my father had gone off somewhere by himself to grieve.

Over everything, however, hovered the imperious and regal shadow of Atalanta. I did not wish to admit this. From the moment she had turned to find my eyes in the church, she had entered my life like a vague promise or a warning. She had admitted me to a different, more acceptable realm. Music was there, and a soft, sad eloquence which came as much from the movements of the body as from the words spoken. A teacup, nestling in its saucer, became filled with meaning; the sound of a door opening was the announcement of the beginning of great tragedy or revelation. The colours of flowers held disturbing meaning, just beyond reach.

And there was the mystery, impervious to my fumbling investigations, of Atalanta herself; the faint vocal accent, the unimaginable delicacy of her hands. She was a carved thing, or something born out of fire and air, drawn out of the heat of a kiln. I sat beneath the Unknown Soldier and thought about her; was I slowly inventing her, as I had done with Agnes? Would the hour come when Atalanta too would reveal her frailty and crumble before my eyes into human-ness? Then I recalled the night when I had been drawn towards discovering the photographs, I thought of the music, the trace of it lingering in the air like perfume . . .

I had been moving towards Atalanta from the start. I knew that now. It bore in on me, a warm revelation, and I was content with it. The soft-hard beating of my heart slowed to a quiet pulsing metronome. It was all quite clear, really; the outcome was not so clear, could not be, was part of the mystery fundamental to our knowing each other at all. Atalanta had come to help me transcend a world grown cruel and remorseless before I'd had time to adjust to it, filling itself with pain, grief, dead dreams, before they'd had time to assume some sort of relative connection to my experience.

Atalanta had moved towards me, probably from the very beginning of time, from remote regions where she too had been advanced upon by fate. Fate in the form of Reginald McKinley, handsome enough in his middle and later age, commanding a certain power, hands that dismissed and beckoned the world. She might have found such things attractive. But she knew, certainly, that McKinley and she would be together; just as, now, sitting under the shadow of violence and war, I knew that Atalanta and I were meant to be together, for however short a time, to share whatever it was that had been assigned to us.

I looked up and it seemed as if I'd been dreaming. The square, the buildings, were transformed into more absolute and demanding degrees of geometry and colour. The square front of M'Whinney's shop seemed to stand out from itself, assume itself again while remaining part of the whole; the reds were redder, the blues bluer, the shape of a car at the side of the square was either frightening or soothing, bold and angry or mellow and smiling. In my nostrils, odours I had not been aware of before, shimmering and quivering there, sharp, bitter, icy.

I tried to stand up, but found myself nailed to the stone, weak enough but warm and cosy as if I'd been immersed in a warm scented bath. I longed for a brush and paints to mark down forever the incredible brilliance of the changing, refocussing, re-imagined place.

Then a hand appeared, huge, hairy, glistening with sweat, and it offered me a glass of water. Shadows danced and played leap-frog on the surface of the water, and longer, immensely dense shadows gathered around me as I drank it. There were voices, heavy, murmuring, threatening and discussing. I could not lift my head; the stones of the gravel surface of the road loomed large, triangular, full of enormous peaks and canyons within which, I knew, whole civilisations had their day. I could peer down at them from the distance of universes, constellations; I swam above them, aloof, not concerned but always curious.

'Let me,' she said.

I knew it was her, I didn't bother to seek her out among the faces that clustered like huge dark moons above me and around me. I allowed myself to be taken on her strong, feathery wings upwards into the rarer air of my own height. Then there was the smothering, breathless heat of the car, the smell of leather scorched by sunlight, the blinding indifference of the sun through the windows, off the bonnet of the car, flashing angles of light like swords – terrible and punishing swords – thirsting for retribution.

'I was just thinking about you,' she said. 'I'm beginning to believe we're fated to meet.'

I crawled halfway between luxurious sleep and a soft, blind terror. Then simple nausea, the movement of the car, the growing pain on one side of my head, forced me to sit up straight. I was in the front seat, beside her, obvious and frank as a boil on the top of my nose.

'I'll open a window,' Atalanta said; and she did; rolling her door-window down, the draught of air immediate and cooling on the back of my neck, the pain in the side of my head beginning to throb, and the gates of her driveway drawing nearer and nearer.

I dreamed.

A boy, naked, stood on a deserted beach and raised his arms. He held the sun in his hands and brought it down, lowered it with infinite care. The sun was like a huge fiery football in his hands. It did not burn him. He crouched down and the sun sizzled at the first touch of the sea. Then it went out and the boy stood up and ran along the beach, into a muttering and ominous twilight.

I opened my eyes and the throbbing at the side of my head had dulled. I was lying on the couch in the room with the piano. Incense burned, I could see its snaking ribbon of smoke curl, round the chairs, over the piano, along the floor. There was no current of air in the room, and the doors to the garden had been closed. My lips were dry. A light embroidered sheet lay over me. I could distinguish dragons and deep green trees. Not a sound entered the room. I felt snugly alone and could not move. Perhaps I should add that I did not *want* to move. The room, the air, the sheet – everything seemed so fragile that any movement of mine might shatter it. There was an acceptable notion that everything had been encased in a very thin film of glass.

After a long time I removed the sheet and tried to stand up. The shock at finding myself completely naked held me sitting on the edge of the couch. I realised that Atalanta McKinley must have undressed me, though I could not recall any period of unconsciousness long enough for her to accomplish it without my knowing. Nevertheless, I sat quite naked on the edge of the couch until I began to shiver. It was strangely cool in the room. I wrapped the illuminated sheet around me and stood up, bare feet plunging into the deep and soothing pile of the carpet.

I opened the door and peered into the wide, high-ceilinged entrance hall; odours of polish and motes of dust floated in sunbeams through the front windows. A lack of sound that was more, weightier, than silence – a vacuum from which all sound had been sucked; my feet struck the cold reflecting tiles of the floor as I made my way across the entrance hall towards the bottom of the stairs. It was a voyage of instinct; other doors, silent and mocking, stared at me from around the hall, but I was not tempted, or led, by any of them. Paintings, shiny, old, imperative things, leaned over from the dark-green wallpaper and sneered. Old men in curled wigs – Handel figures – twitched rolls of important papers and adjusted their robes; lids of tombs moved and argued, stone against stone, the old men leered down, lips thin. Here a fragile woman seated with a mangy dog on her lap, a thin wicked smile on her lips; there, a tall young man leading a horse, or what appeared to be a horse, it was in brown shade; the young man watched and frowned; here again, an elongated painting of a man in white gaiters, a three-quarter-length jacket enclosed in a sash, a short wig with a tail tied in black ribbon, one leg cocked forward cheekily and a sword hanging beneath his arched elbow. The expression on his face was remote, but not unkind.

At the bottom of the wide staircase, banisters immaculate white, two carved marble heads, eyes blind Roman-style, stood guard, wearing their hook-nose arrogance with blind-eyed disdain. They'd stepped straight out of my old Ancient History class, propped up by pomp, Empire, dusty crucifixes; blood in the *arena*, a word the Spaniards still used for sand. What was it the sculptor had deliberately prevented them from seeing?

Dead, smooth, the eyes led nowhere, showed no soul, emitted no light. They stared towards the great door of the house as if expecting their sculptor to return, restore their sight.

I found myself staring at them as they blindly stared at the door. I had no inclination to move, suddenly. I did not know any longer where I was; I knew I was in the McKinley house, but that is not what my confusion meant. Something had slipped in time, or a crack had appeared in the wall of my existence and I had slipped through.

Beyond, dead-eyed Roman heads whispered to me, the marble lids fluttered and bright blue balls of light grew and matured in the cold marble sockets. Suddenly I looked at the heads at the foot of the staircase and their eyes gleamed back at me. Their lips – pudgy and used to good meat and wine pressed from warm grapes in vats pungent with purple grapeskins – parted and tried to press secrets on me, seductions. Dirty old men. I pulled the sheet around me and tried not to look at them any longer, they had almost succeeded in hypnotising me. And that was the secret of their blindness; it had the power to entrance and enchant. Was it a holy, coveted thing, bestowed on them by sculptors who were also magicians?

I climbed the stairs, aware that the rest of the house fell away behind me, and I was suddenly too frightened to look back, as if I had climbed to a dizzying height. Above me, a huge and shining portrait of a medieval hunt scene: a tapestry, a girl led a unicorn and men on horseback pursued a prancing stag through a forest of thin trees. Beyond the trees, a river of silvery thread, boats, men fishing. The tapestry was weighted down by a thick brass rod through folds and little brassy rings at the bottom. I had seen this stag hunt, smaller, more compact, before. I remembered the teacup, my first visit. The theme of the hunt seemed to flow naturally from its miniature drawing-room state to this grander, more noble vision at the summit of the winding stairs.

Where the stairs turned, I looked back. The entrance hall had disappeared. Now that I was close up against the tapestry

I saw that it was very old, the pennants bearing words in Latin and French – I could not make them out clearly, their colours had dulled and blended – flicked and swam against an ice-blue medieval sky. If it was true that medieval pictorial art conveyed messages in symbols, what uncracked codes lay at the heart of the hunt scene? Why, for example, did one of the hunters appear to lean from his saddle and address someone who was out of the picture, to the extreme right? Why did a girl on foot lead a tiny unicorn about the size of a small dog, by a thin gold chain? Who was the woman, side-saddle, her face veiled in white, who rode unobtrusively off to one side, ahead of the hunters but seemingly not racing with them, an observer, anonymous, sinister? On a distant hill, reached by a twisted road, a walled town complete with castle. Above the blue sky, in the heavens, fat, unlikely angels looped banners and delicate fronds of palm back and forth over the world and some puffed out their cheeks and blew against stubborn unmoving clouds.

I knew that, if I tried, I could step forward into the tapestry, become one of the participants in the hunt, discover the identity of the veiled lady. I knew at once how the tapestry had been peopled, how it had been devised, and that once upon a time it had been blank, an unspectacular square of cloth, until the curious stepped nearer and it invited them in. The lady on the horse, snug behind her veil, was no stranger to me. I had pursued her – *would* pursue her – forever. Always she would rest a little distance ahead of me, out of my reach, tantalisingly obscure but known to me even when I slept. I had given her names and might rename her as the hunt went on. It would not matter. I looked at her on the tapestry, aloof, patient, having eternity to play around with, while stags and unicorns, her companions, were hunted or led for her pleasure.

I moved away from the tapestry just as the lady on the horse raised a sliver of finger towards her veil. I was not ready to look upon her. I gathered up my sheet again and moved on, feeling like Lazarus who knew he had no right to walk among the living, annoyed at indiscriminate resurrections, concealing his peeling flesh.

My heart thudded its familiar nerve-wracked tattoo and at the same time I was growing impatient. My head cleared and I did not want to linger in the house. I wanted to find my clothes, get dressed, get back to myself. It seemed that even tapestries on walls conspired to rob me of whatever sense of myself I possessed, threatening me with vague secrets, puzzles, symbolism I could not decipher, yet all of which held clues to the someone else I was becoming. I wanted Atalanta to step up to me and slap my cheek, tell me my father was waiting for me, worried, at home. But I knew such a thing would never happen. The world inside this house did not commune with the world outside it. The rules were different here. I felt a growing anxiety that I might find myself trapped forever inside this brooding house like a fly in a jar, slowly suffocating from a lack of recognisable reality; while at the same time growing euphoric and snug in the gathering dreaming darkness.

And I heard the music, thankfully, about then.

It crept under a sturdy white-painted door down a hallway off the top of the stairs. The walls of the hallway were, as I'd come to expect, dripping with painted eyes and curled wigs, the McKinleys having seemingly been possessed by the notion of preserving their ancestors in paint. I moved towards the door as if the music drew me there on a wire line of sound. Then I realised that I was not hearing music, but something else, a human sound high-pitched, leaping and out of control. It excited me, that sound, its complete erratic fullness. It brought back to me the warmth and frenzied expectation of furtive moments in the bathroom; but it was more than that, deeper, more resonant. I wanted to look upon the source of this music. My hands were sweating and I felt heavy and big between my legs.

I leaned gently against the door. It opened softly, as if it had been meant to, as if there had never been any intention to lock it. It was a bedroom, crammed with ancient toys, old paintings in broken frames littered along the walls, books with thick peeling covers, and in the middle of this disused and dilapidated room, a wide, confused bed upon which Atalanta lay, quite naked, her head strained back and her body writhing, legs motioning like pistons, her hands between her thighs. A musky, earthy odour hung in the room.

I saw the empty bottles stacked in martial rows at the foot of the bed; I saw the great peacock's feathers tossed about the crumbling armchairs near the window with one tragic pane of glass that looked out on the sun-shattered lake. I heard, as a soundtrack to all this, Atalanta's pealing shouts, her rising screams; and the names, one after the other, which she chanted between every hot shuddering breath.

I looked at her and knew that she had become oblivious even to the room, with its acrid smell of decay and fustiness and other things, its destroyed and humbled elegance. She was no longer there, but travelling elsewhere, in the company she had forsaken or been dragged from. Suddenly her hands worked with one seemingly furious effort and she opened her mouth and there was no sound, no music, just an eloquent and exhausted wide-mouthed silence. She held her back arched along the spine and raised off the bed for what seemed like a very long time; then her whole body subsided, all breath pushed out of it.

I began to close over the door, move back into the hall, aware that I was trembling from head to foot, slightly nauseous, that something was over.

As I closed the door I heard Atalanta crying to herself. I knew she would come downstairs in her own time, show me my clothes, possibly make tea, be the polite and ordered lady of the house. I knew also that she too constructed her own versions of reality in order to live. That was her secret: that, and the contents of those bottles, which seemed to help. I did not feel like an intruder on some very private intimate ritual. I felt, oddly, that I had participated in it. That I had been meant to be present in the silence of the house while it took place. I could not shake the feeling that Atalanta had meant me to be there, to discover the unlocked door, to peer in, and that she had been aware of my presence while she carried herself away – as I often did myself – to where nothing existed but one's own body, reacting, aching, creating itself over and over again. It was as if a secret and irredeemable bond had been made between us.

I sat downstairs in the drawing-room waiting for her to compose herself and come down; the most disturbing remembrance of the scene was the rows of bottles, their ridiculous neatness, at the foot of the bed.

For the first time in my life I felt the despair of sharing a secret with another human being. There was no redemption for me now. All innocence, all pretending, had to be done away with. Witnessing Atalanta's self-immolation on the ruined bed had been a kind of initiation for me. I knew that I carried the means to recreate that fire, that self-destructive all-absorbing craving, and that my time would come to use it. I would be in possession of my most destructive weapon. I would reach out with promises and touches and caresses and mould another human being into a creature, monster of divinity, as much in my own likeness as possible. I knew in that moment that every human being in the world possessed and used this power to the same end always.

But then, and always, came the time when the creation found itself, fought for its freedom, declared its independence; Atalanta, writhing in her memories and anguish, conjured up visions of the people who had created her and longed for their caress, their promises again. She had never fought for anything. Never been anyone outside herself, always a novelty devised by other people. Her beauty had not helped.

I saw these things, whether they were true or not, and I believed them and understood them and felt my innocence peel away until my core remained; palpable, raw, prepared. I resolved there and then never to be anyone's creation, to be myself whatever that might turn out to be. It was not much of a resolution, but it was the best I could manage, sitting once again on the edge of the drawing-room couch, shivering and trembling, rubbing my hands, filled with feelings of all kinds so strong that I thought they would drown me. Proud navigator of my destiny, I shivered and thought of a woman.

Seventeen

Early in the morning, buntings nattering with the crackling flags in the windows and strong, deep shadows tossed into the corners by the rising sun, serious-looking men in brushed bowler hats and immaculate white gloves began to appear in the square.

My father, who had no interest whatever in politics and even less in tradition, knowing only his loss of the sea, eggs and later the politics of natural seasons, came to watch because everyone else did and because these were his people and he had done so since he was a boy.

The Unknown Soldier looked even more determined, surrounded by cars with their engines warming up, the sun sparking off the heating metal, doors opening, a soft odour of petrol in the air. The men in their brushed black bowlers adjusted their purple-and orange sashes over their shoulders and fiddled with the polished silver Lodge numbers and the little occult insignia, tiny hammers, swords, dividers. Black shoes, polished to a shining perfection; trousers with knife-sharp pleats, stiff, white collars that chaffed the neck. They looked now and then at the sky, inspected it, commented on how fine a morning it was, and one by one slipped into the cars waiting to take them to Belfast.

There was an attractive childish gaiety about them, out for the day, allowed to be children decked out in arcane ceremonial, proud and shy under the crackling bunting. They laughed and looked embarrassed. Everyone was looking at them. Comment flew back and forth across the square. An explosion of laughter would turn heads. Women made last minute adjustments to a sash here, a collar there, and then stood back and admired their men. M'Whinney looked awkward in stiff black and he toyed with his sash as if he couldn't find a better use for his fingers; I looked around and recognised faces from a more mundane daily routine, life without celebration. The sashes, the bowlers, the day itself, had transformed these everyday people into something special, granting them a unity, an innocence of belonging which was more than ancient commemorative ritual. M'Whinney, and then Agnes' father, Big Bill Fielding, known for the size of his hands, chatted together and shifted themselves on their feet like self-conscious schoolboys on a sports day, togged out and afraid they'd show themselves up.

'Stop footerin' and get into the car,' someone said. Big Bill Fielding looked around and could not trace the source of the voice. It came again, '*Over here, ye bline big woman ye!*' A wee man in bowler and sash and pinstriped trousers held open the door of an impossibly tiny car. I couldn't see how M'Whinney and Fielding would fit. Big Bill widened his eyes; I could see Agnes in him, a wary attractive devilish canniness. '*Stick you in the boot, Geordie! Only you'd drink all's in it!*'

A gust of laughter. Flags quivered and sang along with the blue-and-red-and-white triangular buntings. Glove-studs winked golden in the new sharp sun. The square grew warmer, I stood against a warming stone wall and inhaled the smoke of Gallahers Blues, M'Whinney's favourite cigarette; he'd taken off one snow-white glove to smoke, not daring to taint it with nicotine. My father chatted softly among them, moving from one to another, sea-eyed men, shop-owners. Big-armed women shoved lunch-packs and flasks into the cars after their men and warned them not to get full after the march. *You know me*, the men would shout back; *you know my form*.

Something made me look around the square; no, Atalanta McKinley was not here. This was not her kind of thing. I saw her asleep in that destroyed child's room, muttering, dreaming, while the curtains wheezed against the windows and the lake shivered in the morning sun. My friend, I thought. My mysterious and dangerous friend. My stomach rustled, as if a little animal had come out of hiding there.

Someone blew his nose loudly. Across the square a monkey-like old man in his bowler and sash made himself ridiculous with a few prancing steps imitating the rhythm of a march. *Keep you in the car in case you pass away on us, Fergie!* someone shouted, and the old man stopped, frowned, looked around but could not fix his eyes on the offender and muttered under another hail of laughter. I remembered McKinley's funeral and the dank, final smell of new earth turned under the spade. One by one the cars revved up and moved out of the square towards Belfast. Hands waved and there were more taunts and shouts. There was no malice, no arrogance, no superiority in anyone, just a feeling of liberation from the daily round and a boyish enthusiasm for display and public revelry among other boys. A banner was stowed away carefully into the back of a van, its golden tassels trailing lightly on the ground; the hooves of a horse showed as they handled the banner in, and the numerals *1690. In Pious, Glorious And Immortal Memory;* words shoved into the back of a van with hasty care. The square emptied amid shouts and whistles. 'Will you come back and have a cup of tea?' my father was asking someone. 'I will not, I've nets to mend.' My father looked at the ground. Then the bowler hats moved one way and he moved another.

Eighteen

Ordinary events conspired to increase the sense of unreality which accompanied me almost everywhere.

The Twelfth of July parades through the centre of Belfast – down Royal Avenue, fife, drum and banners fidgeting in the breeze – came to me across the airwaves, through the television, and lacked any solidity or purpose. I saw the little men struggling under the fantastical Lambeg drums and imagined the blood on the drumskins; I saw the fat women wrapped in Union Jacks prancing in front of the white-shirted young lads who tossed the silver-headed maces high into the air with incredible circus-like nobility and ease; I heard the shrill notes of flute bands and the roll and threat of side-drums, but it was all happening in another world. Not a matter of miles down the road. And certainly it had nothing at all to do with the boyish, eager men we'd seen off that morning in the square. It was bigger than they were, it was more grown-up.

My father worked in the kitchen, made sandwiches, his brothers came over and sat for a while and went away again, nursing great silences. They occupied the room with black crowish gestures, breaking the light streaming through the windows, confusing the hot air, making me oddly nervous. They were my own relatives, and I felt threatened and smothered in their company. They were suddenly too big, too clumsy, too much of a presence. I chewed my father's rough ham sandwiches and excused myself. As I left the room one of my uncles belched loudly and threw a question about tides into the room like a challenge. I went for a directionless walk in the barley field, keeping as close to the edges as I could, and when I got back my father's brothers had gone.

I sat on the doorstep, listening to the odd vehicle pass by and fingering slips of grass, trying to make them hum like reeds in my hands, drawing each one close to my eyes and hypnotising myself with the closeness and the fascination with the universality present in the blade of grass. I found something comforting in the thought that someone might well be studying the blade of grass upon which my world and I rested; some vast entity whose eyes were bigger than the universe. Was this what men had come to call God? Some curious and enormous extra-terrestrial, with no greater knowledge of life than I had myself? A fumbler? I found myself drifting from these thoughts into darker ones of tombs and nibbling worms. These days I was full of a sense of mortality and endings. The sun slapped the top of my head with an insistent rhythm and burned the backs of my hands. I ate a quiet fried tea with my father and the evening news carried the sound of drums and flutes again.

I washed the dishes and tidied the kitchen, aware that my father, lulled by the meal, tended to drift away quietly and quickly into reveries of his own. I thought he probably deserved them. I put everything away with an infinite and neurotic care and fell abruptly into an almost physical boredom. Evening dripped over the fields like slow honey, sun-deep, still hot and airless. I took up my little book on Handel and went out through the back door, my father dozing limp-

eyed on a fat chair and tiny flies flickering in and out of the
rooms, crazed by the heat, in search of water.

The yard, as I moved through it, murmured vaguely of
childhood afternoons transfixed by the magic and promise of
broken radios, big-faced and poignant in their valveless silence;
worn and thready tractor tyres, enormous and dangerous-
looking, which you set rolling along the road and then
attempted to jump over, riding high on the slow-moving circle,
being carried over the top; a cricket bat, cracked at the handle,
brining back to me the smell of linseed oil and the noise of
leather on wood, the run up to the stumps, the disputes over
LBWs, Andrew Bell; a flattened red plastic football which bore
no memories but sat sadly in an endless pool of stillness, like a
great flattened forgotten sun; creels, from a time before I was
born, fly-blown and useless, holed; fish boxes, more practical
things, splintery and threatening, *Ardreagh Fishing Co-operative*
inked vaguely into the wood, the staples breaking out, nipping
the air; a sofa, spitting springs and stuffing, broken-backed,
leaning back like an old man at a football match, no longer
quite able to communicate with the game, confused but still
present; albums, Lion, Tiger; a roll of linoleum, like the barrel
of a cannon, protruding from the grass; and suddenly,
mischievously, two curled-cornered photographs. I picked
them up, their backs mildewed, and where they had lain two
fretful tiny spiders scuttled to safety in the rest of the wreckage.

Two photographs: one of a man and two women standing
in front of an ancient black Ford, sunlight shining brightly on
its surface. The man wore baggy pants and braces and stood
feet apart and his hands dug into his pockets; the women, long-
skirted and wearing wide hats that seemed to flap stubbornly
in a breeze, stood on either side of him, smiling also, wearing
that same kind of ease and confidence that Agnes had always
worn when talking to me, an uncaring and diffident air,
arrogant and offensive.

To the right of the group was a palm-tree, bent back on the
same breeze that troubled the ladies' hats, and the sea shone

beyond. I turned over the photograph; scratched in pencil in a very neat hand was the inscription: *Maggie and our Josie and Friend, Malta, 1934*. Nothing else. I looked again at the figures, the man and the women; he was their friend, whatever that meant, and he no longer had a name. His grin knifed out at me, daring me to investigate him. His dark hair was plastered down with hair oil and I imagined intolerable heat, cold drinks, postcards home, and a kind of ceaseless whispering noise always at the edge of everything.

The other photograph was of a confident, smiling young man in shorts and humpy sun hat, one foot on a train that stretched into a mountainous and shaggy distance, his fat suitcase sitting upright on the sandy ground, dark-skinned bearers with fragile thin legs grinned in concert at the camera, and the impression once again was of intense heat, an unspoken discomfort, and vague purposes long ago forgotten.

On the back of this photograph a hand at the very least similar to the other had scribbled in black ink: *Jimmy – Ranjipur R. Station. A few days before his death*. There was no date, no year. No clue whatever to what had happened to Jimmy at or beyond Ranjipur R. Station. The photograph was a mystery, as was its companion. They leered at me, confident of their security and secrecy. They whispered quietly of personal pain suffered in rooms stiff with solitude. Of the tinkle of useless teacups and a pious pouring-in of sugar, just enough to sweeten, while bees turned and looped in small gardens and a bell pealed childishly in a church tower.

Perhaps my father knew the answers, could solve the riddle of these photographs.

I slipped them in between the pages of my book on Handel, aware of what photographs could do and that they lived forever the events depicted in them and that on certain nights they sang a song of infinite loneliness and distress, of events and people forgotten and betrayed by forgetfulness.

I stood out on the road, smelling the hot evening tar and allowing bees to flit past me, plucking the air into a soft humming sound, a note which hung there lazily, tempting harmony. I began walking, comforted by food and feeling dreamy. The photographs had worked like a magic formula on my imagination. I wanted to tell someone about them, have them deciphered; or decipher them myself in the workshop of invention. But I started walking and drifting and the evening stretched out before me like a promise. I passed glasshouses winking with sunlight in green fields, rows of trees that hushed gently in the salted breeze. The fields lay quietly under a hazy blue indefinite sky and sloped towards the sea, littered with gulls. Barley slanted and waved like hair; the threshers were ready, warming up in invisible yards, oiled and hungry.

I stood in the middle of the road and looked behind me and saw the spire of our church, and some of the roofs of houses and buildings, and beyond them the thin white feather of the lighthouse at Ballyhanna and the sea again. I felt, then, that I could dip my hand into the earth of these fields and pull up a familiar part of myself: an arm, a leg, a sliver of soul. We had been here forever; my own family, everyone I knew, had an invisible vein plunged deep in this peninsular earth. History was not sufficient to explain us. We had become this small place and had no other. I saw nothing in that moment that could ever threaten me or become my enemy. I felt a part of the spinning earth as truly as if I had been a tree rooted to it.

The feeling did not last, but moved on quickly like the sad little turbaned men who called now and then at the door selling needle-threaders. My mother would always buy something from them, recollecting afterwards how worn their suits were and how lonely they must feel so far from home. I knew they held the secret of Ranjipur, that they heard it from the bearers who littered the station. My well-being was replaced by a heavy and delicious anguish. I knew that one day I would be merely a photograph, a smile on paper defying explanation. Nothing was certain: the world spun round and round, but its endless rhythm promised nothing.

I began to feel cold, though the evening was hot and breathless. Ghosts seemed to move in the trees now, and the fields were too broad, too silent. I stopped and turned back towards the roofs, the church spire, to familiar things – afraid suddenly of the natural silence of the world and the distances into which men disappeared, smiling, on trains.   '

Nineteen

May 1710.

*Georg Fridiric, aged twenty-four, rocked and shivered in his
carriage; his only companion, a clergyman, was snoring. He pulled
back a soggy velvet curtain and observed a dripping stone world,
unpeopled, unfriendly and mountain cold.*

*For comfort, he patted the rolled recommendations, heavy with
splattery ink and ribboned pomp, which promised a future of sorts.*

*The clergyman, a black shadow rocking in a corner, snored on.
Iron wheel rims grated on slippery cobbles – a street, a village,
somewhere. Georg Fridiric remembered Italy. It had been too easy,
the air was sprayed with doubt. In Florence, upstarts had muttered,
not without reason, about the bits and bobs of borrowed elaboration
his music – they alleged – contained. They could not hide from him,
his Italian was better by the day. He had written nearly a hundred
Italian cantatas, chamber music, a couple of operas – he ran the
list over in his head. They could mutter as much as they liked. In
four years he had risen above the ordinary run of his
contemporaries; they would speak against him, it was irritating but
natural, he was damningly young. Venice, Florence: the art, the*

table talk, a gradual reputation as a wit – where had that sprung from? – were surely enough to uplift and reinforce the spirit of the most melancholic man on earth.

But he had not been uplifted. His spirits still plunged into strange, grey depths and rose as naturally into vague, unreasonable heights. He thought of his father; a room reeking with medical smells, the barber surgeon – an old man when Georg Fridiric was a child – urging a dispeptic little boy in the direction of the profession of lawyer. He thought of his mother, always young to him – three decades younger than her husband, for that matter – and his throat tightened with an indescribable and sudden sadness. He thought of his youngest sister Johanna; she wrapped his letters in pink ribbon, she'd written, and kissed each one. He had written to her, to them all, and felt not one bit better for it. Homesickness dogged him in Italy and he had confided this to no one. He had sworn viciously, been drunk too often. The Italians, foppish, tittering, had stared gape-eyed at his volleys in their own tongue, laughing behind their hands when his solid rural German accent corrupted its rhythm. Perhaps too much bile and longing had seeped into his music. He recognised well enough its flaws, its tendency to drag elegantly. Perhaps what they praised – and they did, in spite of everything and rather outlandishly – was his loneliness. Back, now, a man of the world, written testimonies bulging from his pockets, to Hanover. But he could not bring himself to speak of triumph.

The carriage squeaked to a stop. He longed for the company of a woman, the warmth, the physical momentum. He groaned against the unseasonal mountain weather. He twitched again at the sodden drapery and saw this time an open door, a ragged figure brandishing a fizzling torch.

The clergyman spluttered awake. Georg Fridiric inhaled the tang of gin. The man struggled into consciousness, then put on an absurd act of straightening himself into respectability.

'We've stopped,' the clergyman said.

In the damp darkness of the carriage, Georg Fridiric sighed. He closed his eyes and saw a woman's face, the features contorted and unrecognisable. A trickle of guilt, no more. Her image vanished and he saw his father again, twisting his hands, an argument raging between them, the flames of the fire climbing higher and higher in the enormous hearth with the earnestness of their words.

Words swam in the rainy air. The driver's seat creaked and a spring pinged; the driver was dismounting. The clergyman was wiping his mouth with the back of his hand. He struggled into a wide black hat. But for his pale, sickly face shining in the gloom of the carriage, he would have been invisible.

The door on Georg Fridiric's side was jerked open. Cold and rain blew in. Clearly, it was intended that they should get out. The figure in the doorway brandished the torch and signalled Georg Fridiric and the clergyman towards him. There was warmth in the doorway light. 'I won't risk an axle,' the driver was saying. 'I know what happens, I've seen it. Your roads are a peril to life, Sir. As God is my witness.'

The accusation seemed to be directed at the figure in the doorway. He took no notice, but beamed a smile at his two guests. The driver and his side-kick, meanwhile, began unloading luggage. Georg Fridiric fretted for his manuscripts, but was lured by the heat of the inn.

Inside, a fire roared brightly and a table was being set out with rough wooden plates by a fat woman in dirty, wide skirts. Items of clothing hung on a cord near the fire, newly washed, but giving off a stale, pitiful odour. A great crucifix with a dilapidated and one-armed Christ hung precariously over the fireplace. Smoke belched in noisesome sooty gouts out of the great hearth's mouth. The stone flagged floor was covered with old straw. In a low, intensely black doorway, a child stood, wide-eyed, filthy ragged hair hanging in clotted lengths over its face. Boy or girl, he couldn't tell. Bare feet crossed one over the other. A filthy greyish shift hung on a thin, shivering body. Georg Fridiric managed a smile, but the child stared back expressionlessly. The room, he noticed, was chilly, in spite of the fire; vapour wafted from his mouth. The room smelled of old wet clothes and unwashed bodies and choking wood smoke. Nothing of the golden rooms of the Teatro San Giovanni Crisostomo here! Winter in Venice; cold, mist, boats like corpses bobbing in the murky lagoons, marshes and fever, the influenza which was almost fashionable to die from. But style, seductive style! Scented kerchiefs, powdered bosoms. Music, always music. They had no complaints, none of them. Now this: a mountain, a torrent, a child in rags and a drunken cleric!

Georg Fridiric was seized by one of the fits of unreasoning panic he'd suffered since as far back as he could recall. One couldn't tolerate such abrupt transitions in one's life. He didn't want to be stopped, high in the mountains, between nowhere and nowhere, alone, sad. Movement helped. If only they'd kept going, he'd calm down. His breath shortened. He sat down in his wet, now gently steaming clothes.

The clergyman had vanished. Trunks and valises thudded into the room. The fat woman produced a candle, lighted a torch. Flicks of yellow light threw gargantuan, apocryphal shadows on the peeling plaster walls. Horses whinnied and coughed outside under the rain. Georg Fridiric thought he was about to be overwhelmed; his heart pounded, his throat was dry and felt as if it were closing.

The clergyman clambered like a black crab back into the room, wide-awake now, holding a pewter mug of steaming hot mulled wine in each bony fist. Perhaps the man had sensed something unsettled in Georg Fridiric.

In any case, the rough concoction did the trick. He calmed down, felt warmed, sleepy. Hammering sounds came from the street, then curses. The fat woman returned and placed rough country bread in front of them, stained knives, a jug of vinegarish wine and a pile of fatty beef. She smiled at them. There were no single rooms. There were no guest rooms at all. Georg Fridiric would lie down under the table with the clergyman, if that was all right. There were blankets, of course. She vanished again, came back with a pile of dubious sheeting. All the time the child stared from the black doorway, now and then picking its nose and shoving the findings into a dripping nostril. Another mug of steaming wine and a few slivers of meat and Georg Fridiric didn't particularly care.

Later he undressed to his underwear in a shadowy corner of the room where the light from the walled torch and the fire and the spitting, withered candle couldn't penetrate. The clergyman remained seated at the table, drinking, still in his damp clothes. In his shift, Georg Fridiric arranged blankets beneath the table and near the fragile heat of the fire. The coarse, uneven cloth smelled of shit. He lay down, wishing the clergyman a brusque good night.

'I am dying, Herr Handel,' the clergyman replied.

Georg Fridiric propped his head on an arm and thought of Hanover. He saw now how worn and stained the cleric's black *wraps were, how grey and fingerprinted his neckerchief. His appeal pricked the background, like an out-of-pitch singer in a choir.*

I am very sorry, Georg Fridiric offered. He knew he should have said more, or at least have been prepared to listen. But he was tired, a little drunk, and afraid of his nerves acting up on him again before sleep came.

'I have done nothing with my life,' said the drunken cleric. 'Saved no one, brought no one to God. I am going home to die.'

Georg Fridiric imagined a tragedy, a music, that encompassed the man's life. Everyone's life had a music that described it. It was merely a question of uncovering it, allowing it sufficient space in which to compose itself.

In the midst of these not so unpleasant abstractions, Georg Fridiric saw the clergyman rise up, a black collossus against the ceiling of the room, and strike down at the table with one of the unwashed knives.

The cleric let out a terrifying yell. Scuffling in other rooms announced the waking of the innkeeper and his fat wife, probably the carriage driver and his second. The place was coming alive, the clergyman's yell had woken it.

Georg Fridiric tried to remove himself from under the table, cracked his forehead savagely, heard voices in the room. Now the innkeeper, in his night-clothes, was trying to take the knife from the drunken, death-enraged clergyman's fist. Now the carriage driver was dancing around both of them, red-faced and useless. Suddenly the clergyman let go of the knife, lost his balance, toppled backwards and danced, arms spinning in a vain attempt at retrieving balance, into the fireplace.

With a roar, he sat in among the flames. For an instant, he seemed to make no effort to get out of them. He looked like a vision of a prophet tested in the flame.

Hands rushed to pull and tug at him. His clothes were smouldering when they dragged him to his feet, the room was filled with the odour of singed hair and burning cloth, the innkeeper's fat wife was screaming uncontrollably. The child did not appear.

Alone now, dog tired, Georg Fridiric allowed the rocking of the carriage to calm him. It was a bright morning and the wooded slopes, invisible in the night, looked peaceful and reassuring. He tried not to think of the poor clergyman and the constables who had restrained him, angry men called out to the middle of nowhere on a wet and blowy night. There were fears in his own head that needed restraining. Music achieved that, to some extent. To some extent not.

Alone in the carriage Georg Fridiric awaited the return of his familiar melancholy, the tightening of his throat. Now and then he fingered the slightly damp parchment upon which recommendations, words of princely praise, inked sighs of approval puffed and preened. The carriage seemed to descend. He couldn't, alas, fight off the vision of the clergyman seated among the flames; an apocryphal figure, a myth made flesh, a one-man opera. Then Georg Fridiric's tightening throat relaxed suddenly. He giggled. He saw the clergyman wide-eyed in the fire. He began to laugh. He could not stop himself. He felt ashamed and bewildered. He laughed and laughed, tears running down his face. The carriage rocked and rocked downhill. Georg Fridiric wept hysterically and longed, like a gape-eyed, shoeless child lost in a dark place, for his mother.

I sat on the grassy verge of the road and I imagined him, young, frightened, alone, moving towards Hanover.

I turned back the pages, reading again to myself the anecdote of how Handel's father had forbidden him to play an instrument, how Handel's determination, as I read it, encouraged him to smuggle a clavichord into an attic room, where he went when the house slept, and where he played in spite of the world. The story meant something to me. Its significance escaped me, but I felt proud of Handel and of myself every time I read it.

The photographs and the book I carried in my hand like a hymnal. Now the fields had darkened and there was the usual shiver of ominousness about them, as if they had been kissed by poisoned dark lips. Birds, invisible, cawed and cackled in the trees. Evening waded in from the sea with steady deliberate strides. I walked more quickly. By the time I reached the first houses of the village stars had pricked their way out, blinked uneasily, tested the firmament. The book snuggled into the hollow of my hand, bending slightly, assuming an arc. A man's life in those pages. It seemed so easy and so quick. You started at his birth and you told every story that led to his death and that was that.

The moon rose, heavy and pocked like a Spanish orange, the same colour too, up out of Kintyre, cold and uncaring and full of itself.

Twenty

My father spoke less and less about my mother, as if she was slowly ceasing to exist with his withdrawal of words. Our visits were embarrassed outings; we sat together in the front of the van and talked about football matches, the local team's chances in the League, this sort of thing. Driving out of our country into the other place that Belfast was, with its incriminating hints of violence and its restless, gable-painted streets. United only in that we were going to visit the same woman, my father and I often sat in a thick syrup of hot silence, the sun mauling our faces and the leather of the seats and the fields folding back on each side of the little van like flimsy, coloured carpet. We had nothing more to say to one another on the subject of my mother's illness; and its sinister terminal resonance didn't encourage discussion.

My father's face was smaller than I'd ever noticed it before, smaller than a dried-up apple and just as wrinkled and hollow. He'd lost some of his hair and aged by a hundred years in a couple of months. He hated to be in the hospital if my mother's relations, brother and sisters, were there; he seemed to think they blamed him for something. Courteous people, devoid of malice, they lurked in the corners of corridors and haunted the door of the room like ghosts. I wondered if they too had photographs taken in hot climates, secrets preserved forever on paper.

My father sought refuge in his refusal to discuss my mother or her condition; he had begun to do a kind of penance. We always left the city of Belfast in half-darkness. Once I saw a young woman in a short skirt chase a man into the road, waving her handbag at him. Her lips moved soundlessly on the other side of the windscreen of our van. The young man stood out in the middle of the street and put his hand up for a taxi. 'Pay no attention, son,' said my father, and we drove on. He'd seen it too, and I was surprised he had.

Then came the day when old men down by the harbour retreated into their myths and muttered about a smell on the wind, a change in the way birds circled the quay, lights seen at night floating on the surface of the water like souls.

I sat, alone, among coiled ropes and the smell of tar and oil, taking in the immense melancholy of the little harbour and the slow rhythmic working of men on the half dozen boats. Here and there, an uncle, yet another brother of my father. They'd raise red hands and wave at me. Their work absorbed them like a sacred and ancient ritual. Here a man uncoiled rope while another mended the tattery squares of netting; wooden fish crates lay everywhere or stood stacked in uneasy piles on the slippery stone flags of the quay. Names printed in hasty blue dye: *Ardglass, Castletrevor, Clogherhead*. Diesel spread a thin coloured film over the flat, calm water in the harbour, imprisoning shattered boxes, empty cigarette packets, bits of rope, shards of crates, and sad-looking feathers. Seagulls, open-mouthed, screamed in circles over the boats, lying wings outwards on invisible steady lifts of air. Fish-heads lay on the planked decks of the chubby boats, eyes wide to the world of dark sea. The men on the boats worked in knee-high boots and thick sweaters and clucked to each other in their abrupt old

Scots accents. Now and then words like *cran* and *fash* came up to me like verbal offerings. I knew that I turned my words in the same accent, pronounced my syllables with the same flat knife-sharp cut. The boats' aerials flapped lazily in the breeze and now and then the soft warm chug-chug of a generator sounded under the conversations and the squally croak of seagulls.

Always, the odour of fish and oil and tar; I looked over the harbour and felt at home, and more than merely that.

I knew these men around me; even those that I didn't know and were not relations, they were part of me as I was part of them. We had moulded the aching coastline and ploughed the sliver of sea between here and Scotland, harvested it, for generations. Our names sounded in every tiny graveyard along the coast. Over wee unimportant shops; in the registers of churches whose front doors needed repairing and where ivy claimed the cracks in the pebbledash walls; we had set down our nets here and hauled up ourselves for longer than we could remember. A knife dropped on stone; the sound of iron on rock; a man's laughter spilling over the flat water; the vomity splash of a bucket being emptied overboard; sounds that filtered into me as much as the sounds of crows in fields thick with new seed.

I closed my eyes and allowed sound only to take me over; it washed into my blood and took up a language only I knew. To part me, or any of these men, from their labour or their land was to drag the pumping heart out of a living body. I opened my eyes and saw the names of the boats: *Angelina,* for my uncle's wife; *Maid of the North,* for a man who'd married a girl from Belfast; *Sally Ann,* for a man whose two daughters were named Sally and Ann; legends attached to every name, every boat. They were not just vessels of timber and iron; they too had souls and histories. And I was thinking this when, in a boat named *The Star of Mourne,* for a long-dead owner from the foot of the mountains, they arrived with the body of a young woman.

Twenty-One

The Star of Mourne was a fat trawler built in the high-prowed design of boats who found themselves often in the deadly waters of the Irish Sea.

Her lines were perfect, and every unnecessary angle and decorative twirl had been honed away; she was smoothly curved, almost sensuous. The way her bows beat up and down in the water made me stare at them, that seductive slap into the water and the slow rise out of it.

Men stood wide-legged on her front deck and figures moved in the cabin and on the four-windowed bridge. In other boats and working on the quay, watchful men seemed to be waiting for her. Now, several cars had slipped on to the quay; men were accumulating in knots everywhere, not saying much. *The Star of Mourne* lurched abruptly into the flat black harbour water and birds rose up and searched the decks for fish with their wide eyes.

Some of the men on deck wore the uniforms of policemen and seemed unsteady on their feet. An ambulance worked its way through the growing groups of onlookers on the quayside. Women wrapped themselves in long dark coats and whispered to each other over their collars. *The Star of Mourne* was tied up in the harbour and thick brown diesel smoke belched lazily from her exhausts. My father had arrived, on the far side of the harbour, he couldn't see me. Walter Smith was there, and some others I knew. Walter saw me but refused to come over. For a silly moment or two we eyed each other over the harbour.

I was seized with a notion, an idea, a fear, something I could not put a proper name to. I stood, beginning to shiver, between big coats and men who squinted their eyes to see through the glare of the sun on the water. I edged my way out slowly and started making my way around to *The Star of Mourne*. I had to be careful; I did not want my father to see me and call me back.

On board the trawler a stretcher was passed forward. It was covered with a rough grey blanket and looked very thin and flimsy. The old men on the quay nodded to each other; they had, once again, read the omens right. Women gasped, then pretended to turn their heads away. A body had been taken from the sea and it was everybody's business. Who was it? A stranger? Someone we all knew?

I made my way around the harbour and was standing at the top of the stone steps between ambulance men and some local police when the stretcher mischieviously threw off its blanket. It flapped open like the wings of a skate and glided down into the oily water. Slowly it seemed to take flight, struggle upwards for a moment on a current of air, then become absorbed in the water silently, without fuss, where it changed colour and lay a few inches below the water's surface, a jellyfish now, no longer interesting to look at.

But now I was staring at the face of a young girl. I was staring and everyone else was staring, and the women were the first to groan; a sound which turned upwards into a wail. The blonde hair was matted and flung back; the pale skin of the face had turned purplish and transparent and one of the blue eyes was missing; I could see that the eyes were blue, for one stared open upwards into the hot sky.

The face laughed silently, loudly. The lips had been drawn back from the teeth of the open mouth and the upper lip had deteriorated as far as the beginning of the nose. A tiny mischievous crab about the size of a penny scrambled out of the open mouth and disappeared beneath the body. After their brief instinctive keen, the women stared at the face, the older ones used to seeing the savaged faces of the sea-dead. The rest of the body wore bits of a skirt, bits of a pullover, and the legs revealed bone and cartilage the colour of fishmeat, almost dissolved. I turned away and vomited and felt my father approaching me. *Get the lad away,* I heard someone say. No, I told myself; I would not turn away from this. I would not get sick. I straightened up, saw my father coming, saw them load the body quickly in the back of the ambulance, and made myself invisible, weakly, in the crowds that followed it as it lurched out of the harbour.

The work on the boats resumed. Everyone trickled away. The face was more or less unrecognisable anyway, and that put an end to speculation for the time being. No one had gone missing locally, that was agreed. But I could not explain the fear which had overtaken me, forcing me to make my way round to see the face of the body. And the blanket had obligingly floated into the harbour. The corpse no longer knew shame.

I sat on a stone bollard and waited for the sun to dry my terrors and my fear. I seemed to *know* death now. I knew its face. We were rapidly becoming good friends. I saw her car then, the widow McKinley, the last to leave the harbour, going up slowly behind the stragglers, patiently driven, in no hurry. She had been here all the time and she had ignored me. All I wanted to do was go after her; she seemed to know when I was at my most vulnerable. She seemed to know things about me even I did not know.

I dreamed again, a slow, unsteady dream.

It took shape gradually, as I awoke from it and, miraculously, returned to it. The face of the drowned girl surfaced through the darkness, fled past me, returned and went again. I was down at the docks. Then I was somewhere else, the wheat and barley fields blazed, my father spoke to someone whose face I could not see. *The Lord Giveth and the Lord Taketh Away*. Then it was night; or perhaps I should say, a darkness descended, a biblical, thick darkness full of silence. I was walking into the living-room, the piano mute and patient to one side, everything dark except for an edge of bright light which seemed to slit the darkness open like an envelope. There was a delicate and unplaceable perfume, as if someone wearing scent had just passed through the room. I was drawn towards the widening span of light. And immersed within it was Atalanta, smiling, holding my book – *her* book – on Handel in one hand, beckoning with the fingers of the other.

I looked at my own hands and saw that I held photographs in them, fanned out like playing-cards, and it was impossible to make out what was portrayed on them, the scenes shifted constantly. Atalanta stood now in the yard behind our house, the barley and wheat fields waving like grey hair in the bright moonlight. Her smile was constant and unchanging. I wanted to touch her face; the photographs fell from my fingers as my hands came up. Then I was out in the yard too, feeling the early morning chill, the tickle of breeze in my hair. Atalanta moved her mouth, formed words with her lips, but no sounds came out. I moved closer, she placed her hands on my shoulders and I felt an embarrassing warmth spreading over my chest, belly, between my thighs. I was hard, erect, embarrassed. Atalanta whispered one single word: *sleep*. Then I was falling backwards and she was moving upwards into the black and suddenly moonless sky.

I seemed to fall with a kind of tangible thump on to the big armchair. I had managed, in my sleep, to walk to the living-room and sit down; my thighs and fingers were sticky and wet and the tang of ammonia and salt rose up from them like acid, burning through my embarrassment, making me stand up, rush about in the dark looking for tissues. I didn't want to wake my father. I didn't want him to find me there, as I was. I forgot about the dream that had, somehow, led me there and offered me something I'd managed to lose on waking.

As I moved about I began to feel the onset of longing and sadness. I knew that when I looked I would find the back door open – what was out there? Dreams? Only dreams? Or nothing at all but the breeze over the fields? I felt the cold air on my moist thighs as I opened the door further. The moonlight flooded the fields like a helicopter searchlight. Did it probe the waving stalks of barley and wheat for some sign of Atalanta? What did the moon look for in the fields?

A puffy burst of strength filled the breeze, and something crackled lightly like the first flames of a fire, at the edge of the yard just beyond the door. I looked around, then down, noting the stillness and sharpness of shadows, the remorseless dedication of shapes obscured by night.

A book.

The pages flew open in the breeze, the covers snapped back and forth. I bent down, knowing before I did so what book it was. Handel. What Atalanta and I had in common; the book that was the key, the thing that joined us, if nothing else did. It should not have been there. It had been on the chair beside my bed, where I'd left it before turning out the light. I'd been reading it in bed.

The book did not try to explain itself. It rested like a wounded and grateful bird in my open hands. I felt my heart extend its rhythm, pick up speed. My hands were clammy now, and my forehead melted in a cold sweat. I could not explain the presence of this book there, outside the door, under the night. I felt a rising and smothering fear that seemed out of place on the back step of my own home. But it was there, rising upwards, clawing at me, trying to drag me down with it. And the fear itself terrified me.

I ran back into the house, not bothering to close the door. In the dark of the room I fell against something and toppled over. It was a long, black fall to earth.

Then I woke up. In bed.

For real this time.

Twenty-Two

The kettle whined childishly, full of steam. The sun cut a thick angle across the kitchen floor and the table. Marmalade, butter in a dish with the wrapper still on, two mugs for tea, my father's with a chip out of the rim, the white hill of sugar in the glinting glass bowl, the blinding spark of sun off knives and spoons and forks; and over everything, the odour of eggs frying and dip-bread and treacle-farls blackening under the toaster-rings.

The sun was on my neck as I sat waiting for the plate of eggs, bacon, dip, potato-bread, farl, the kind of breakfast that was meant to set you going for the day. The tea came hot and thick, poured by my father with his shirt-sleeves rolled past the elbows, shirt open-necked and the smell of shaving-cream still hanging around him. He looked well, his movements sure and not as creaky and anxious as they often were. He reached me the envelope and when I saw it was opened I knew he'd read what was in it and didn't feel upset. I noticed, when he leaned forward, how his thin hair was still parted straight down the centre of his scalp and how he must have looked in the days

101

when he posed for the kind of photograph that now and then seemed to slip into my life like a hint of something. Handsome, in his conservative way. Dark eyes, a fisherman, standing with his hands deep in his wide trouser pockets and his feet well apart, balancing perfectly.

I poured YR sauce over the eggs and potato-bread because I loved its catch and tang on my tongue and the soft exotic mixture of egg-yolk, yellow and liquid, with the various sauce-spices. It woke my mouth up. Saturday mornings were special. They had a different weight to them than other days. Time was different. The sun did not run as swiftly over the heavens. The air was newer. There had been no night, nothing before. Everything was just about to happen in the world. I sugared my tea twice and stirred and my father sat down at an angle to me and buttered some Hovis. Without looking up, his hands moving methodically buttering, he said, 'You did your best, son, and that's all you or anyone else can ever do.'

He went on buttering, slap-and-slide, and I unfolded the list of examination results and saw that I would not go to university in Belfast or anywhere else. My heart beat faster, even though my father's calmness should have calmed me. Then I looked up at him and his eyes went into mine.

He spoke through a mouthful of bread. 'You could always go on at the Tech another year and try repeating some of them. But I don't know if you'd want that.'

I did not know if he had asked me a proper question which required, right there and then, an answer; perhaps this was just a prelude to some great and terrible anger and only an answer would stave it off. My mouth was full of yolk and YR and the taste of tannin. A car engine stuttered up the road, I could feel the yellow sun burn the back of my neck. I hadn't washed myself yet, there was night still in my eyes, a dusty, gritty feeling. My heart slowed down. 'No,' I said, 'I don't want to go to the Tech for another year, Da.'

And we kept on eating until out plates were cleared, until we had both mopped up yolk and sauce with dry squares of

Hovis brown and drained the teapot. 'I'll clean up, Da,' I said, standing up before he did. He sat back on the chair and placed his hands on his belly, locking the fingers. For a moment he seemed to stare at nothing, some vague point on the table, some middle-distance of the soul or heart. Perhaps he saw something coming back to him, or going away from him. I could see his tongue moving against his cheek as he sought to dislodge something from his teeth. 'Don't you bother, son,' my father said, 'go wash yourself. Are you coming to the match with your uncle Isaac and me?'

Slowly, as time passed, I was beginning to enjoy standing on the football terraces between them less and less; always there was the feeling that perhaps I should have been somewhere else. These days, that 'somewhere else' had a geographical location and a woman's name. He knew nothing about that. I felt that I owed him something for being so good or restrained or whatever he had managed to be about the bad examination results; I'd fallen down on Mathematics, Physics and Geography and that was enough to end it for me.

So I said, 'Yes, I'd love to go'. which was more enthusiasm than I'd ever shown him for a Saturday football match and he must have known it. He smiled, still investigating his teeth with his tongue. 'Say nothing to your Ma, I'll tell her in my own way,' he said. I knew then that it had been important to him, that he had controlled his feelings for my sake. Why? I was never to know. One aspect of my father I could not understand, why he should suddenly spare my feelings and be gentle with my ambitions.

I had hours to spend alone with myself and I did not want that. On the road I met Walter Smith, who also had had bad news. His father had asked him if he wanted to start on one of the smaller fishing-boats, that he might be able to arrange it for him. Walter, devastated, and with Agnes on his mind these days, hadn't much to say for himself. Suddenly our misfortunes became potential for friendship. He walked along with me for a while, then turned back. I watched him go, a small insignificant figure dissolving in the sun, no danger to anyone. There was a generous lump in my throat; something had been revealed to me, but I could find no name for it. Dreams, photographs, my mother, father, Agnes, examination results, Walter – everything was part of a whole and at times it was too much to take in. I ran over my list and wondered how I'd managed to exclude Mrs McKinley, Atalanta, and all that had happened, for what it was worth. Something had blocked her out. Was she the only real thing in my life?

I was walking up the McKinley driveway, the elephants drawing closer, the house bathed in sunlight and its own fragile silence. I saw her car and I saw Atalanta, rising up slowly from the ground where she had been trowelling or digging. Her face was shadowed by a large hat. She wore loose-fitting denim jeans and a flimsy shirt.

I was insanely, desperately in love with her and that Saturday morning I knew the pain of it.

Twenty-Three

Dust. There was dust everywhere. Motes glided and swung in the sunlight. There was the acrid smell of dust, a dry, thin smell. In the hallway, on the banisters, the busts, the mythical beasts, the blind eyes.

I waited for her, the front door open, in my hand a glass of whiskey I'd poured for her when she requested it. I stood there, not knowing what to do next. I sniffed the whiskey, reeled back from its fumes.

Then she came in, trowel in hand, her wide hat slipping sideways, that inviolable smile. Her eyes seemed to gather up all the light that was in the hallway, in the garden, the fields beyond. Today she was in fond, almost happy mood. She took the glass out of my hand, sipped furiously, handed it back to me. 'I can tell you're in a rush,' she said. I heard the faint traces of an accent again, and again wondered where she came from and how it was that, with all my intensity, I still knew so little about her.

Today I felt like confiding whole parts of my life to her; the results of my examinations, my thoughts about that, my mother's illness, how it made me feel. Even Agnes. I wanted to tell her about Agnes and the changes that had come over her. But there seemed not to be an opening. Then again, all those things seemed to belong to somewhere else.

She took off her hat, allowing her hair a flowing eager freedom. She beckoned me into the sitting-room; more dust, on the piano, elsewhere, as if the entire building was beginning to disintegrate with a slow, fine delicacy, like the ending of a symphony, all parts correct.

'There is never enough time for anything these days,' Atalanta said. She walked away from me, I inspected the contours of her body. The power of what I felt embarrassed me. I waited until she had leaned against the edge of a big armchair. 'I saw you down at the harbour when they brought in that girl,' I said. Atalanta looked into her glass. The liquid sat, gold and silver mixed, waiting for her lips. Yes, I thought; I saw you. You did not get away unnoticed. 'Why were you there?' I asked her. 'I heard about it,' Atalanta said. She was nervous, mobile. Her eyes stayed looking into the whiskey. 'Sometimes I can feel these things happening or about to happen. It's something I inherited from my mother. It is a gift or a curse, depending on how you look at it. The air suddenly thickens, birds fly excitedly here and there . . . there are a hundred different ways of telling. I can tell. I knew there was misfortune at the harbour. I went there and you know the rest.'

I listened to her explanation and tripped suddenly into the black, deep well of a thought which frightened me. 'Did you know who she was?' I asked her. And I watched her, scared, not wanting to have her say yes.

'No,' Atalanta said. 'No, I didn't know her. One cannot ever *know* someone, anyway. Didn't anyone ever tell you that? Does that answer your question? Or do you think I murdered her and threw her in the sea?'

I smiled, but I was not comfortable with my thoughts. I felt, rather than heard, the incredible and sudden silence of the house, the weight of sunlight suddenly oppressive and smothering through every window, every opening past a door. It lay everywhere, hot, yellow, stiff and thick like paint. 'I did not murder anyone,' Atalanta said. Her voice was deeper now, the whiskey already in it and flavouring it. 'What horrible thoughts you have about me! For shame!'

'I don't,' I said.' I don't have horrible thoughts about you at all. It's not like that.'

Atalanta smiled, sipped, smiled over her glass. I remembered her on the bed, her almost animal selfishness and self-absorption. The picture disturbed me. I could not look at her. She rose from the side of the chair and came towards me. She put the glass down. I smelled a faint odour of cinnamon.

'Give me your right hand. I won't eat you! Give me your right hand. Let me see your palm.'

She took my hand in her fingers, her touch ran up my arm and made me shiver. Cold. Atalanta's fingers were incredibly cold. Cinnamon and the sharp odour of whiskey on her breath, the hair in a swarm around her face now, her eyelashes hovering over her face like the wings of an insect.

Carefully she drew the nail of her index finger around the palm of my hand. I felt my erection grow, tremble. I stepped back from her. She followed me. I stepped again, her finger drew itself over the faint lines on my palm and an absurd dance began. My hard erect penis rubbed against the inside of her thigh no matter how I tried to prevent it. Then she drew back suddenly. 'A long life-line,' she said, 'how many of us can say that? In love, I see many beautiful girls. Some will break your heart. Others will have their hearts broken by you. You will travel much but never leave your own country. You will never be rich. You will earn your living by writing. Do you write?'

'Yes,' I said. Her finger traced my future; my penis crumpled and died. Her exploring finger-nail etched itself through my future years like a scalpel through thin skin.

I lay exposed there, without secrets, vulnerable. My heart beat a silly and loud tattoo which I was certain she could hear.

I looked down her blouse at the abrupt and creamy rise of her breasts and thought of McKinley, so much older, dominating her and making her do things that made her utter the kind of noises she'd been making in that bedroom. I blushed. All was heat, around, within me. She dropped my hand. 'Tell me what you write,' she said, and retreated to her drink and the big armchair.

I told her about the play I'd written about Agnes. I told her about Agnes, about Walter, about Agnes' pregnancy. I could not stop unfolding the great quilt of my life. I spread it out there where Atalanta could see and judge its worth and I no longer cared. I told her about my mother's illness, how I felt so very little about that; and how much pity I'd begun to feel for my father as he tried valiantly to keep up emotional appearances.

I told Atalanta that, in honesty, I could feel him die a little each day. I didn't know if I loved or even liked my mother. I told her I did not believe in the world, hadn't really believed in it for a very long time, longer than I could remember, and that I had odd dreams which were lovely and sinister and overwhelming all at the same time. The world was not real to me as it was to other people; my father suspected, or at least had gone through a time when he had suspected, that there was something wrong with me. Perhaps he was right. But as time went by, whether he was right mattered less and less to me, I told her. I would leave here eventually, I would take my vision or my daft and useless dream with me, and that would be that. I did not know precisely the nature or function of that dream, there was no use in her asking me too much about it.

But I knew that it had something to do with my ability to transform Agnes into a Lady for whom Knights waged war, in a land where bushes and trees glowed at night and turrets could be heard whispering to one another.

Explaining all of this sounded silly and ridiculous; I had invented a whole country, a whole culture and a language when I should have been doing my homework and my father had told me to destroy it, it wasn't healthy, and I had done so. Now

I realised that I should not have been so hasty. I did not believe in the world he believed in. I should not have given my world over to his so readily.

I told Atalanta that I had never been so explicit with anyone in my life as I was being now right there with her. I didn't know why. She made me feel that, somewhere, my voice would be met with similar voices. I was not so terribly alone. My one dread was that I might wake up from a dreamless sleep one day to discover that I no longer believed in my dreams, that they were the property of someone else, someone more worthy of them. When people said things like *He'll grow out of it,* I felt the damning possible truth in that and sensed that I too was doomed to lose what was valuable to me and replace it with things I did not believe in at all, yet which were considered to be necessary for the proper conduct of my life. Just as she sensed things about to happen, so also did I, but in a different way: I saw life as a set of symbols and linking coincidences. Behind every ordinary and mundane event, a magical story unfolded simultaneously. How silly, I told her! How could anyone live like that? But how could anyone *fail* to live like that?

'Agnes was your Lady,' Atalanta said, 'but she has fallen from grace. She has become human. How dreadful!'

'I suppose so,' I said. My outpouring had exhausted me. I began to think of the duty of going to the football match, how much I wanted to stay where I was with Atalanta and my opened heart.

'Now you have fastened your dreams on someone else,' she said. 'And this other woman walks without her feet touching the ground, shines like silver through the fields, music accompanies her wherever she goes?'

'Something like that.'

'You have tasted love's essence but have never loved,' Atalanta said. 'Not properly, not with fire and steel blades in your heart, not like that. You must not be in such a hurry.'

'I just don't ever want to end up like my father,' I said. I heard myself say the words and they frightened me. I had betrayed my father in one sentence, had cut forever a silken thread that bound us together.

'You don't think he has ever loved as you do?' Atalanta said. 'You think he does not feel love now?'

'I don't know,' I said. 'I don't know what he feels. Desperation, I suppose. He haunts that hospital. I don't ever want to suffer like him, to live all my life in one place and then to suffer. It's not right. There must be more.'

'You don't respect him anymore, is that it?' Atalanta had come over to me, spoke softly, her voice embracing the air, closing the distance between us.

'I don't know what I feel for him, one way or another,' I said. 'Because I don't even know what I feel about myself. I want, sometimes, just to run away, go off somewhere where nobody knows me, start all over again.'

'Ah, yes!' said Atalanta. 'I know that feeling very well. It is not as easy as that. The world is too small, or perhaps our imagination is too small. Or perhaps we simply grow afraid of change, much as we desire it.'

'Please don't tell anyone else anything I've said,' I pleaded, aware now that I had spoken secrets, heart-deep things the relevance of which I could not quite identify myself. A first step of sorts had been taken, I was quite aware of that.

Atalanta put her hand on my shoulder and smiled at me and the whiteness of her teeth and the soft wetness of her mouth made me quiver inside.

'Does anyone know you come here to see me?' 'No,' I said. 'Let's keep it a secret between the two of us,' she said. 'Our own secret, our own treasure.' 'Yes, yes,' I said, aware that my voice had softened to a whisper. Her arms were around me, pulling me towards her, then embracing me tightly. My face buried in her hair, I could smell her hair and the light soapiness of her neck. 'Our secret against the rest of the world,' she said: 'and you can reveal to me all the hardest things, the most unreachable things, the dreams, all of it. You are my secret as I am yours. Do you agree?' 'Yes,' I said. 'Yes, yes.'

She released me. I was crying, yes, I'd somehow thought I might be. I felt foolish in front of her. She handed me a paper handkerchief and waited until I'd blown my nose. Then she showed me to the front door. She was standing at the big door as I made my way down the driveway, I could feel her gaze on me. Perhaps at my next visit it would be her turn, and I would learn all there was to learn about Atalanta McKinley. I was bitterly thankful that I had restrained myself and had not revealed anything of how I felt towards her: a growing need which could only be quenched when I had conquered my own terror and touched her body.

I came out of the driveway and started along the road home. I was thinking of how much I'd told her, or how much she had managed to get from me, and I was thinking of the loss of my father, how I'd given him up in a single sentence, perhaps forever.

The van was on top of me almost before I saw it. My football mad uncle Isaac and my father stared out at me through the windscreen. The van stopped, my father got out. 'Do you realise what hour of the day it is, lad? We nearly left you behind.'

I saw my uncle's unmoving bowl of a face peering out at us through the windscreen.

'I went for a walk, Da.'

My father looked over me, over the listless hot trees to the almost hidden distant chimneys of the McKinley house. Then he looked down at me, then up at this guilty horizon again. I stood there in the hot road, smelling the melting tarmacadam, the hedges, hearing the occasional abrupt buzzing of bees, the steady thrumming of the van's little engine.

My father's brows dipped and narrowed. He poked me sharply on the side of my arm. 'Where did you go for a walk, my lad?'

'Just walking,' I replied. My heart betrayed me, bumping and jumping again. This is what I wanted to escape from, the interminable questioning, answering, being accountable. The eyes of the world united over my father's eyes. Had he discovered my secret, Atalanta? He looked over me again and then scoured my face with those ancient, deep methodical eyes of his. Through them also generations of fishermen looked, accusing me.

'Get into the van, and you'll tell me in future where you're off to.'

I climbed in behind my uncle Isaac, a vast shape in a brown pullover. We started to drive off. My father squinted into the sun and scrutinised the driveway leading to Atalanta and my secrets. 'What's up there?' my father asked, addressing no one, knowing the answer. 'The McKinley house,' his brother replied. I caught my father's eyes in the rear-view mirror. I gathered up as much courage as I could manage and held the gaze. 'Are you starin' at me, boy?' my father said, more harshness and anger in his voice than I'd heard in a long time. His brother's silence enhanced it.

'No, Da,' I said, drawing my eyes off his, looking out of the window at the fields, the sun flashing on the glasshouses, the swoops of crows and seagulls. I was right to betray you, I thought; I have to, if I am to survive. The van hopped and bumped and made me nauseous. I knew a silence had begun to grow up between my father and me which would come and go, interspersed with impossibly good mornings and even occasional intimacies. As time went on, the silence would take over everything, muffle all closeness, smother our friendship and make us two separate and different people.

Strangers, in the end. Nothing in common but our name.

Twenty-Four

Always nervous in crowds, I looked upon standing at a football match – up there on the windy terrace among the black caps and cigarettes – as a kind of ritualised public test of myself.

I had never been able to refuse to go. As a very young child, I had laboured and sweated among the forest of legs and the heavy swing of thick coats, running off to pee under the stands in the welcome anonymous darkfuls of urine smells. Here I could recreate my legends, don strange hats, be many people, heroes and villains.

Always at the heart of my stories lay a mystery of some kind which I, as hero, set out to unravel. Often I reckon my father didn't notice that I'd gone, cemented to a terrace along with his brother Isaac, shouting, getting annoyed, arguing the toss with whoever stood beside him or looking round, as spectators always do, for some sort of collusion.

Now I stood between my father and my uncle Isaac, as tall as either of them, anxiety a fire in my belly, my eyes searching for runways through the crowds, always on the edge of an obscene vague panic.

The smell of trampled earth rose into the terraces even on days when the earth was rock-hard. The sun lay over everything like a blanket and there was no wind. The turnstiles, *creak-creak*, smelled of old sweating iron and the wee invisible man giving out the tickets coughed hideously. Smoke blew back like scarves over mens' shoulders. Hands in pockets, or leaning on the blood-smelling rail, everyone kept up a steady bantering conversation with themselves and the players, who could not hear them. Everyone thought he was controlling the play. There was a stake for everyone. No one was disinterested. The players slid, had whistles blown at them, scored goals with heavy applauded thuds of leather on leather, saved goals, jostled one another, all under the administering eye of the spectators. For ninety minutes each man was God. Heroes rose, fell. A roar went up in the stands high above us, men sitting on hard wooden benches privileged and out of the glare of the sun. Whenever it rained, the odour of wet cloth dripped over everything like gas.

I was there, on the terraces, waiting for an opportunity to cheer and rid myself for a few moments of the building tension. Even here, I was not one of them, not a part of what was going on. Once, when I was about twelve, I'd read a copy of *Amazing Stories* about how Martians had created people who looked like humans and set them down on the Earth with memories just like other people; terrified, I'd shown the book to my father and asked him if I was one of them. Surely, that day on the terraces, I was the only one in that entire crowd who was thinking of Georg Fridiric Handel.

I carried the book on his life with me everywhere. In a land of covenants, this was a token of my covenant with Atalanta. Without it, I thought, I would have lost her. Just as a woman, losing her wedding-ring, might feel.

'Are you okay?' my father asked, looking down at me suddenly – I'd unconsciously slipped down a few terrace steps. 'Aye,' I said. 'I'm fine.' '*Come back up here!*' 'I'm fine here.'

I wanted to slip away. I wanted to read. No chance. I was being watched. They suspected something, the eyes on the house. Referee! You're like a big wummann! Aukawayyon! Referee! You're *bline*! You big *stewmer*!

'The Famous Saxon', Scarlatti had called him; candleglow and the hot smell of wax melting. Order, a shuffling of crinolines, skirts, men adjusting their swords, holding them so they wouldn't clink and clatter. Venice: masks. Titters behind them, Handel a rising star. He too wore a mask, hiding behind it, wishing for a cosy place to sit and think. Enjoying the thing but at the same time a little worn out; twelve months at Florence before this, becoming so well known that it was impossible to buy a loaf of bread without having to endure questions, bowings, people shoved out of the way to allow him to be first served. Lot of nonsense. Flattering nonsense. His temper was frayed.

In a mask, he squinted through the glow of yellow light and watched Scarlatti watching him. A Cardinal swathed in suffocating, immobilising ermine presided from a raised chair. Of course, Scarlatti waited until Handel had been asked to play before formally unmasking him. Dolt! A bit of play on Scarlatti's part to draw attention to himself – guess who I know! This sort of thing was always tedious. Despite himself, Handel felt the glow of acclaim, women's eyes. Already he'd had a few. No paunch yet, slim and eager, blowing out bedside candles while horses clip-clopped past the open windows. Scarlatti followed him – Scarlatti wore a mask with a rudely pointed nose, a facial phallus – from the harpsichord to a dim corner with a gratuitous glass of wine in hand and three hangers-on.

Suddenly feeling very weary, he heard Scarlatti rise to the subject of writing operas. There was an edge to Scarlatti's voice Handel did not much care for. 'Of course,' said Scarlatti, 'one such as yourself, maestro, could not be requested to do anything for nothing.' The way he wheedled over the word maestro made the German cringe. Glass of wine in the face might be the answer. No – no duels, please.

'One is obliged to live, Sir,' said Handel.

Scarlatti ignored the dismissal in Handel's voice. The note of admiration Handel detected in Scarlatti's voice unsettled him.

'Then you think you might honour these citizens by composing a work in honour – that accursed word again! – of your stay in Venice? I know they would not be ungrateful. I for my part would be delighted. It is not every day, you understand.'

Have I misjudged the man? Despite everything, I rather like him, thought Handel. My Italian, though bad, is good enough for librettos and subverting women; his German, or whatever it is he's at, is deplorable. All of it, the effort-making and the humbug, conspires to make him likeable. In a qualified sort of way. But I get his idea. Guilt, if I don't comply.

'Yes, yes, my dear Scarlatti, I had not thought to leave Venice without doing a little something.'

'What?' said Scarlatti. Handel repeated himself, very slowly, Scarlatti bowing his head at every word as if conducting the sentence. The surrounding burghers bowed too. In the hot yellow light, the ermined Cardinal was vomiting into a silver bowl held up to his chin by a wigged lackey.

'Something, something modest,' Scarlatti purred.

'I don't write modestly,' said Handel. Sniggers in the candlelight, yellow flickers on faces; a woman would be welcome now, her flouncy entry would mark my exit.

'In fact, I may have just the thing. Something with a distinctly Italian flavour. Something with a touch of history.' 'What?' said Scarlatti again. 'Yes,' said Handel. 'I'll do it.'

'His Eminence owns the perfect theatre,' said Scarlatti with a flourish of his white-ruffed wrists in the direction of the wretching Cardinal.

Agrippina. Scarlatti, give honour where honour is due, did the flunkeying and arranged Cardinal Grimani's dusty, mouldering Teatro San Giovanni Cristosomo. Scarlatti does not shirk. Carnival time; what is dear Domenico getting out of all this? Surely he doesn't need to rub against me, he who is well acquainted with Cardinals who own theatres and have rooms of precious paintings, all the way to the ceiling!

Twenty-seven nights later, worn out by applause, Handel took himself to a dark and beery inn where no one knew him, or cared. Drunk as a lord! Himmel! He stumbled out into the lane escorted by a barefooted doxy and almost knocked his head against the out-swung door of the carriage. Inside, in the nefarious dark, Scarlatti, like Mephistopheles himself, everywhere at once, knowing everything.

A clap of hands. A coin. The doxy disappeared. 'Herr Handel' – that atrocious but somehow loveable accent! – 'these streets are dangerous.' 'There are things more dangerous,' muttered the German. 'What?' said Scarlatti.

All in a dream. The carriage rocks and sways like a small boat on a stormy sea. Now there are fields silent under frost, skies open like blue eyes. Hanover, under a hush of brown chimney-smoke. Spires, sloping roofs; a city. Handel is asleep.

My father shoved me. I closed the book quickly, locked it into a pocket out of sight. Crowds came down like Assyrian hordes off the terraces. The noise, the tramp of feet.

'Waste of time bringing this boy to a football match,' said my father to the air.

A flight of duck, triangulated, dipping, over the harvesting fields towards the reeds, the lough; I stood watching them like an augur trying to divine some sacred signal. In the fields, machines moved with grumbling direct efficiency, swathing through the nodding barley, wheat, leaving wide highways of stubble behind them. Swarms of rats scurried at the edge of the road, in the ditches, frantic, hungry for the spilled grain. The sun, heavy and brazen-faced as ever, blessed us all.

Twenty-Five

I heard the car in the distance and instinctively stood back.

She smiled through the windscreen, pulled up. The door opened, a hand reaching out for me. I needed little encouragement.

She was wearing a flimsy long white dress which formed over her legs wonderfully. A hat of straw, a ribbon around the crown. Eyes alight with the sun and some mad promise; freckles I hadn't noticed before. A smile. That was all. 'Get in,' she said, and patted the passenger's seat, pat-pat. And I did.

Power under us, a surge, and the car broke through the ranks of hustling brown rats and belted on down the hot road, breaking the fragile heat mirages, curving through their glass currents like a sleek blade. Her side window was lowered down and I lowered mine; blasts of warm air around the inside of the car, around my head, throwing my hair into blazing fits. The odour of melting tar and cut grass, the distant growl of big harvester engines. Somewhere in it all, the immediate and responsive tang and bite of the sea.

Today I wore new denim jeans; eighteen years of age, now, a boy no more. They hugged and prolonged my lankiness. But they were what teenagers wore hanging around cafés and lounging on motorbikes in all the most important films. They were what you wore to challenge and defy the world. You could tuck your fingers into the back pockets and take on just about anybody, especially if they were your first pair. These were mine. That day, and those jeans, are one.

'The end of the old agricultural year is close at hand,' she said. 'Now is the time for rejoicing and giving thanks. At least, that was once the thing. Modern times, people don't bother now.'

'We still have Harvest Services,' I said, full of jeans and wisdom.

'Ah, yes, of course, I realise that,' Atalanta said.

The road burned under the car, the engine gears changed, her hand strong and the wrist tight on the lever. I tried not to peer obviously down to where her skirt moved up and over her knees. Skin smooth and sprinkled with tiny blonde hairs. Her hair was tied up under her hat; her neck, paler than her legs, the hairs fair and ragged. 'Oh, well, so many things were here before we put *order* on them. I mean, there was always order, *natural* order. If things were right, we should hibernate all winter. Capitalism ordains otherwise. You don't have the faintest idea what I'm on about, do you?'

I hadn't, no; but to admit such a thing when you're in love is to die. And she burned through me, so close I could smell all the mysterious aromas of her womanness. I was nothing sitting there beside her. Yet I was all things and everything that had ever been and greater than that. She had chosen me, God only knew why, and I was beyond questioning it. 'I think,' I said, 'that you mean we are all stupid and daft for working the whole year round.'

'In a manner of speaking,' she said. Her accent, drifting in and out of something familiar yet remote, foreign yet snugly local. Her lips, I saw, were wet and shiny. She looked away over the fields to the sea. 'What are you doing for the rest of the day?'

'Nothing', I told her; 'nothing.'

'Good. Indulge me, then. Look after me. We'll have a picnic, walk by the sea. Christ! But it's a beautiful day.'

Slight whiff of wine-breath. Well, that would explain her euphoria. I did not understand that, since my own euphoria was natural, other people's could be as well. Everything, even feelings of intense devotional love, were my personal property and no one had any right to experience them without my permission.

The road dipped, we flew past my house. I knew my father was out, driving the van around the place, and I was no longer afraid of being seen with Atalanta. I just didn't want to have to explain anything to anyone. With Atalanta, despite her petty confusions and enigmas, there was an untouchable simplicity. Explanations and probings would destroy it. Ardreagh still frowned on her for not wearing widow's black.

We drove into the centre of the village, rounded the square under the Unknown Soldier, and parked. Odour of hot metal, plastic, leather. I leaned my elbow out of the window in as rakish a fashion as I could manage. The much-reduced Walter Smith shuffled by the long *Bushmills* window of Ernest May's public house, going into the bookmaker's with a sullen, desperate air. Agnes was fat and wobbly these days, her face blotchy and her once-lovely legs gone all stumpy. Beside me, the long legs of Mrs McKinley danced out on to the gravel.

'A decent bottle of wine,' she said, 'some cheese, maybe? French bread? No, you can't get it here. Nearest you come to it is those fat Vienna Rolls. Not the same thing *at all*. Have you ever torn off lumps of warm bread, tasted the salt in it, used it to wipe up your soup?'

Atalanta made wiping gestures. 'Sitting on a Mediterranean beach with a Berber butcher ritually slaughtering a sheep for a get-together when night falls? Luminous surf, hot nights, sand in your hair?'

'No,' I said. I hadn't done any of that.

'Well,' she said, skipping away from the car and slamming the door at the same time – Smithy looked up and over – 'your day will come. Sausage, if I can get any. Do you drink beer? Of course you do. You *dabble*.'

'I'm not allowed,' I said, miserably seeking refuge in the official position. Ardreagh, in spite of May's pub, was reputed to be good-living and drinking, though indulged in on certain ceremonial occasions, was not a ritualised social thing. I had seen my father tipsy. Once.

Atalanta disappeared. Smith wormed his way over the silent square, bringing with him the sound of stray invisible dogs. Mothers wheeling infants seemed to crowd behind him past M'Whinney's shop, metaphors for something. The Unknown Soldier threw his usual premeditated shadow over everything. Smithy looked, above all, tired. Old. Old too soon. He looked past me into the car. 'No flies on *you,* brother.'

Smithy's desolation filled the car like petrol-fumes. But the mad old carelessness tried to tamp it down. 'I bet you're buckin' her. I bet you are.' 'No, I'm not.' 'You *have* to be.' 'Well, I'm not and you can think what you like.' 'What I think is you're buckin' her. Only a fruit'd not want to.' 'I'm not a fruit.' 'You *must* be.'

Smithy leaned himself over my elbow menacingly. The way a whipped dog menaces another dog. The viciousness gathered like armies behind his eyes. He'd been robbed of something. 'I'm telling everybody you're buckin' the widow,' he said.

'You tell anybody and see what'll happen to you,' I said. 'I know that's libel. *Slander.* That's against the law and I'll tell Mrs McKinley it was you and you'll end up in borstal in Millisle or somewhere.'

Smithy grinned. Then he grabbed my nose, twisted it, then my arm, bending it back at an absurd angle against the outside of the car and wrenching me round painfully, inside. I yelled at him to let go. All he kept saying was – *You're buckin' her, you're buckin' her, say it! Say it and I'll let go your arm.*

He looked up, released my arm, backed away from the car. He was looking at something, staring over the top of the car, backing away. I rubbed my arm and looked where he looked. Atalanta was standing about ten yards away, a few parcels in her arms, not quite done. She was standing with the breeze whipping her skirt against her legs, between her legs, sculpting her in wind and cloth. She was staring at Smithy, just staring, her face set, expressionless.

Without moving, then, she raised her chin, smiled, and said, quite loudly, 'Ah, you must be Walter Smith, the young gentleman who made that young Fielding girl pregnant? What does it feel like to be a father against your will, your youth wasted and over, and you a mere ignorant child yourself?'

A few heads turned on the pavement. I felt sorry for Walter. He just kept backing off as if he would back away forever into a tiny point in the universe and finally disappear, grateful to be gone. He looked from me to Atalanta and back again, then turned, vanished into the shade outside the bookie's. When I looked back towards Atalanta she was, of course, gone. There was no one like her in the world, certainly not in my world. I could not have imagined or created her or a character like her. Yet she belonged in the imagination, something about her was too fragile for the world. Did I imagine this? Perhaps. Such courage mixed with fragility was admirable.

I wanted to tell her so. I wanted to tell her so many things. When she came back she was so loaded down with things that I had to get out and help her load up; bread, butter, plastic forks and knives, *two* bottles of wine and a few bottles of beer, slices of wet ham, sausage and other eatables. 'Such a filthy mouth,' she muttered, 'that Smith chap. What sort of parents reared him to be like that, I wonder. I pity any child of his.'

She looked at me without raising her head and I blushed, Oh yes, I most certainly did. In she got; off we drove. I had no care whatsoever for the stares of the pavements, the shops. The Unknown Soldier's shadow lengthened, crows and gulls competed for invisible crumbs under his bayonet, through the fidgety hot barking of stray dogs I could hear across the square the gathering rising commentary of the bookmaker's radio.

Twenty-Six

The car bucked and tilted over the sandy surface of the lane. High lank grasses waved like radio antennae. Seabirds squawked and circled and hovered. When the car stopped, the hot salty air rushed in, a pause in the breath, a hot, heavy, comforting thing. Pages of newspapers, fluttering like broken insect wings, drifted around my legs. Torn headlines; a blurred photo of an armoured-car. News from another country.

Atalanta, skirt sailing and breaking around her legs like water, stepped into the breeze, took off her flapping straw hat, undid her hair, let it play in the salted wind. Instinctively, as all people who step out of cars at the edge of the sea, we stared out to sea without seeing anything, dragged without realising why to its primal heart.

The moon directed us here, as it did the movements of the water; I felt the fluidity of my body shift and pulse and adjust itself to such a proximity of liquid power. The noise of the sea, rolling pebbles in its mouth, and the black roar of wind in my ears and the tingle of hot unadulterated sun on my skin;

Atalanta extended her arms and became a cruciform, spiralled once around, let the wind turn her inside out, smiled at me, dropped her arms.

'God's living-room,' she said.

We carried armfuls of things, bottles, jars, tins, over the needling fine sand. A heat-haze settled on the horizon. Under it, not yet utterly sucked into it, a trawler asserted its image, a painterly afterthought. The car receded, alone in the dunes, dozing off. We walked, made the familiar trudge that walking in blowing sand is, found a place Atalanta thought suitable, sat down. Our bits and pieces lay around the outspreading tartan blanket like wreckage spat out on a bored tide.

Atalanta, legs folded beneath her, surveyed the sea. She squinted into God's glare, sniffed, looked at me as if to make sure I hadn't disappeared. I could scarcely bear to look at the side of her face.

'It was once thought that women had more liquid in them than men, and therefore were more open to the moods of the moon,' Atalanta said. 'There is something appealing in the notion. I mean, if you don't believe in God anymore and yet don't want to feel entirely helpless. Do you?'

'Believe in God?' I said, bewildered and happy. 'I suppose I do. Everyone else does. Everyone that I know.'

'Of course you do,' Atalanta said.

We stared out to sea. I thought of my mother, semi-conscious in a room that lacked everything, even pity, certainly love, in an enfolding darkness that promised no relief this side of death. God was not in rooms such as that, I felt certain. At least, he was not in *her* room. I did not understand everything that Atalanta said and comforted myself that she spoke from some other world, some place where everything made its own sense and to which I myself would come when the time was right. When I'd grown up, if that phrase meant anything. I did not wish to question her about anything, but felt privileged to sit at her feet like a stupefied novice at the feet of a sage, drunk on words and the mysteries they hinted at, understanding nothing. But I wasn't ready to discuss God or my feelings about God. I thought of Andrew Bell. I thought of cricket matches, dry earth and flies and heat, and Welshmen with God for a prop-forward.

'Are you dozing off?'

'No,' I said. 'I'm thinking.'

'And what are you thinking about?'

'Not much. I knew a minister once who was on the African missions.'

Atalanta's face darkened, a sudden and barely noticeable change. I saw the lids of her eyes fall down like shutters, a certain light extinguished. Then they rose again, the light came on again. More mysteries? Atalanta patted the top of my hand in a way that made me wince.

'A very honourable vocation,' she said. 'There's nothing like teaching primitive people the proper way to live. Now – would you be dreadfully daring and try some beer? There's no one here to give you a conscience.'

Conscience and guilt were, of course, out of the question in this tiny island of time and space we had coveted for ourselves. I did not even think of what it would be like to go home to my father with the smell of beer on my breath. I opened the bottle like a man. I slugged too much beer at once, felt the cold-hot smack at the back of my throat, saw Atalanta sorting slices of rough-looking bread to make sandwiches. Beer in my belly and chewing ham and bread with mustard; the sea roared, the birds rose and yelled, the sun licked both of us. It found our secret places, uncovered us.

I lay sipping a second bottle of beer, a towel over my now bare legs and my shirt bundled up like something dead behind me. Atalanta, slugging from a bottle of wine, stood up, appearing enormous against the soft blue curtain of the sky, lifted her skirt over her head as if I wasn't there to watch and devour every inch, the curves, the soft brown hollows and dips, the snowy contours of her underwear, panties and brassiere, my heart speeding and drumming, my blood dominating, my mouth drying up despite the beer. The sun made love to her, stranded her semi-nakedness in pools of syrupy light, drowned her slimness in shadow and then swallowed it in swirls of colour. The vision of her lying on the bed in that broken room, her head tossing from side to side and her fingers working in a mad rhythm; I closed my eyes, feeling the pulsing arousal under my towel, ashamed, exposed, destroyed.

Atalanta slugged from the bottle, cruciformed herself once more as if inviting the sun to take possession of her, then threw back her head, gurgled deep in her throat, a sound I had never imagined a human being making, the sound of an awkward animal. I felt that somewhere in the world, or directly behind me, other animals made similar sounds, called to each other, implored and lamented like this. 'To the sea!' Atalanta cried. '*To the sea!*'

Propped on one elbow I watched her dance, spin, leap towards the sea. Then she stopped, turned, waved, undid her brassiere and slipped out of her panties and even at that distance I could make out the dark triangle of hair between her thighs. Cruciform twirling again, she plunged into the water, running into it, not slowing down until she had the green sea up around her waist.

I lay back, thinking of her, drifting on a cloud of beer and delirium. I cared for absolutely nothing beyond the moment, the beach, the sea, Atalanta. Death without pain, but enveloped in pleasure, *was* possible.

Sand brushed against my cheek; I rose up again on an elbow and saw her play with the sea, fondle its hair, make it laugh. I heard a vague but sad music, and looked around. Nothing, of course. But the music persisted. Was it in my head? I don't know. It was most definitely *there*, soft, poignant, emanating from the earth. I looked at Atalanta in the sea and felt a powerful watery sadness, as if something shuddered and died in front of me, something very close, without which I was lost. Deliberately I opened another bottle of beer and swallowed hard, the glass mouth of the bottle clicking hideously against the wire on my teeth, feeling the intense buzzing in my ears and the swimming in my head increase. The music was everywhere now, soft strings rising and falling.

When I woke up Atalanta was sitting beside me, hair wet, wearing her skirt again, leaning back on her hands, eyes closed, her cheeks reddened by the sun and salt. I looked at her until she acknowledged me. 'You slept,' she said, 'too much beer too quickly. I thought it best to let you sleep.'

And, bending over, she kissed my pimply forehead.

Twenty-Seven

Inside the car again, there was the tang of salt on flesh; not my flesh, hers. I hadn't been able to open myself to the elements and besides, Atalanta seemed to have made the sea her own, and I had little business being there.

In fields heavy with the thick sleep of evening, the big red and yellow harvesters grumbled slowly to a stop. The sun's face was wrapped in a warm furry veil. Birds manoeuvred and swung in abrupt battalions from tree to tree, signalling, scouting, above the world. I felt above the ordinary world too, lulled by a pleasant heaviness around the eyes, not able to think of anything for more than a moment at a time, watching everything.

Beside me, Atalanta drove carefully, despite her intake of wine, hummed a snip of a tune now and then, and occasionally turned her head to me and smiled.

I felt that her kiss on my forehead still burned. Nothing could touch either of us, we were proclaiming our being different to the world. An obscure pride began to take shape; I thought briefly of my father, of lives ordered differently from the way in which they should have, or could have, been run. I thought briefly also of Walter Smith: already he was twice his age, growing older every time he stepped inside a bookie's, a schoolboy still but driven like a nail into adulthood. I knew there was something wrong in that, though I didn't really understand what it was and probably could not properly articulate it.

But I knew there was something wrong and was glad I was not part of it.

And when my father's face came back to me I felt sad, as if he stood on a lonely railway station platform and I leaned out of the window of the carriage and waved to him, moving out, losing him forever.

The square had huddled down now into its accumulated heat. The window of Ernest May's public house squinted in the dying sunlight; M'Whinney's was closed and shuttered, asleep already. Shadows outgrew themselves, too long for the small streets and sloping square. Dogs barked, girls gathered on corners, eyeing everything, animated, hands flying. A couple of old men in caps, leaning on sticks, smoked pipes under the Unknown Soldier. Here and there flowers muttered lazily in window-boxes, pampered, nothing to worry them. The one daily bus to Belfast was gone an hour ago, the townland swallowed it up and dozed to digest it.

The engine of our car whined and echoed around the square, gained strength up past the church, swifts darted like aircraft in a dogfight, straight out of *Lion* or *Tiger* or *The Beezer*. Big strong trees raised high the darkening sky. Our windows were up now against the insects of the evening. Now and then a moth or beetle or something else would smash itself against the windscreen, a tiny explosion, a splash of juices and legs and crust.

Up the driveway – passing my house, I had felt the hot breath of guilt, but it had passed – and the McKinley house seemed to shine in the gathering haze, a mist rose out of the lake behind it, and when Atalanta turned off the car engine, no birdsound, nothing. A deep emptying stillness bathed everything. The blind unlighted eyes of curtained windows gazed down at us.

Atalanta stepped away briskly from the car, slamming the door behind her. For a moment, I thought, she stared up at the house as if she had never seen it before. Then she turned to me, smiled, indicated that I should take out the rubbish we'd made, the empty wine bottle, the full wine bottle, and bring it into the house. I gathered everything as best I could into my arms. She walked on ahead of me, I kicked my door closed with my foot, feeling the weight of stillness touch me gently on the shoulders. I did not want to be left alone, stranded beside the car. I did not know why.

Up the stone steps, into the hallway, and Atalanta had switched on some lights. The stairway opened in front of me like a mouth. She turned off into the drawing-room. More lights. She saw me standing in the hallway laden with my petty burden of picnic things, and came back to me. 'Follow me with all that,' she said.

The kitchen was a wilderness of untidiness, dishes unwashed, pots in the vast stone sink, cobwebs on the small back windows, the red tiles cracked and stained, a fusty, decaying odour clinging to the air and, I presumed, to my clothes after a while. Dish-cloths, heavy with burdens of clotted grease, hung like broken flags of battle off the edges of the wooden table near the devastated stove. Grease and dust lay heavily everywhere together like elements of the same calamity. Blue-mould rotted into bread and knives, laden with lard and butter, stuck hopelessly to surface-tops. Here and there a cup sparkled treacherously and gave itself away. There was occasional evidence to suggest that, from time to time, something like panic overcame Atalanta and she had dived recklessly into the business of cleaning up. These fits had not come often. In a dark twittering corner of the kitchen where a swinging light-bulb, naked and confused, could not toss its yellow stain, a stack of empty wine-bottles.

Atalanta sorted and dumped. The weak sick light of the kitchen – what my father might have called a *scullery* – painted everything with a degree of ordinariness which I found oppressive. I wanted to get out of there, leave her to it, close my eyes and change the scene. I felt tired. There was a thin pane of glass between me and the world. It was not unpleasant. The feeling of floating somewhere above everything was in danger of collapsing in that kitchen. I couldn't wait for Atalanta to give everything up, abandon everything; which she eventually did. Hugging an unopened bottle, she ushered me out of the kitchen.

Across the mouth of the stairway again – I thought of the bedroom upstairs, of what Atalanta had looked like on the bed – and into the bright drawing-room. Through the windows, I could see the last throb of the sun before it vanished.

A crescent moon, thin as a blade, drew itself out of trees and reeds. A single very bright star accompanied it.

Atalanta showed me to one of the deep-cushioned armchairs and switched out the light abruptly, throwing the room into a confusion of shapes and shadows which, for a moment, I found alarming. But I said nothing, feeling a spell of sorts coming on. Smiling, smiling now almost all the time, no matter what she was doing in the thick darkness, Atalanta poured drinks into our glasses. One she handed to me: the odour was sharp, hard on my nostrils.

'French brandy,' she said in the lessening darkness, 'the very best. We must never stop once we've started. Never. It would be a sin.'

I sipped, not wanting to refuse, not wanting to throw up. To my surprise, I did not throw up, but the fiery liquid burned its way gently down my throat and flattened out in my stomach. My cheeks burned. I felt the world, tentative as it was, slipping away. I could not have gone home anyway, smelling of drink. The realisation panicked me; I had nowhere to go, for the very first time in my life. And I was completely in the hands of someone else. Had I relinquished all control over my own life?

Would I never get it back? I sat in the deep chair, my heart thudding loudly, afraid and unable to say so. A cowardly pride.

Music filled the dark room. At first I did not know its source: then I heard the rough and repeated crackling of a record on the ancient player. *Handel.* I might have anticipated it. Pebble-on-the-beach sound of the underlying harpsichord; rushing water of violins, spilled marbles of sound. Frustratingly gentle: the world expressed in terms of water, slow forgiving light, trees that barely moved. A woman's voice. A rising treble.

Atalanta was nowhere to be seen. The music, the voice, rose and cascaded through the dark room, over my head, the fumes of the French brandy and the music tearing me gently apart. I was no longer myself or anything that resembled me. I was changing, metamorphosing, the chrysalis splitting. I was becoming new.

The singer's voice trembled on the peak of a note and fell down the other side. I saw a vision of a sharp-peaked mountain, a figure falling and falling down one side, over and over. Suddenly, out of the corner of my eye, a slash of light tore through the blackness. Then another, then the sound of Atalanta giggling, a sound full of menace in the circumstances. Vaguely now, and reassuringly, I made out the shape of the door to the hallway. Behind me, I knew, the moon and stars were rising higher, prickling the darkness of the lake with white light.

Atalanta went on lighting tall white-stemmed candles in various parts of the room until the odour of burning candlegrease contested sickeningly with the fumes of the brandy.

A curious vulgar heat emanated from the candles. The evening was warm, close. Light shattered everything now into strange untamed reflections. My eyes began to hurt. Too much concentrated light against too much dark. A sudden rush of air bent the candleflames. The windows behind me had been opened. A shape that might have been Atalanta threw itself in a wide arc around the room and there was the soft hush of a door opening and closing.

I put down my glass of French brandy and tried to stand up. Dizzy, I sat down again, no strength in my arms and legs. The candle-heat, the music, soothed me and agitated me at the same time. I felt that I had crossed a line, gone too far. A vague uncomfortable feeling. I wanted, in that moment, to be at home in my bed, reading about Handel.

But Handel's music rounded on me, nailed me even more securely to the big chair. Everything, music, light, dark, heat, smell, combined to smother me. From the first, I told myself, I had been foolish. Atalanta was, perhaps, *too* different. I did not feel good being alone with her, not as I had felt on the beach. Though nothing menacing or frightening had actually happened to me, I felt that I was paying a price for the beach. For feeling good in her company. For feeling good at all. Guilt began to edge into me. I should not be here. Always, the feeling that I should be somewhere else. Surrounded by familiar and comforting things. I tried again to stand up. This time I managed it.

And then Atalanta was standing in front of me, smiling still, her hair replaced by an enormous curled silvery-white wig, a massive shining skirt flowing out around her, making a whispering sound as it swayed from the stem of her waist and caressed the floor. A gaudy necklace swung around her neck and between her breasts. Long, puffed-out sleeves glistened like tentacles. Smiling always. But now the smile was no longer funny.

Atalanta moved slowly into the shivering light of her groups of candles, a ridiculous and sad figure. The long wig seemed to pull her head forward. The wide floating skirt shone with a curious pink light. There was the faint odour of perfume, of mothballs. She stood with the light on one side of her face, flames dancing in her eyes. The hysterical smile never left her face, as if by now it no longer could. She raised one hand and shoved into my face what at first I took to be a human scalp. I stepped back, brandy slopping out of my glass. I looked again, heard Atalanta's laughter. Another wig. Shorter, cropped. A faint powdery glow, curled. 'This is for you,' she said. 'Put it on. Go on. Play the game. Amuse me.'

Play the game. This was some sort of game. I calmed down. The singing rose and fell, great gusts turned into light breezes. 'V'adoro Pupille,' said Atalanta, 'from *Julius Caesar*. Marvellous! You can hear the harpsichord quite plainly. Everything else born upwards upon it. Marvellous!'

In her other hand she carried her brandy glass; she raised it, looked around the room, saw an unopened bottle of wine, made for it, upsetting the *tableau*. She scrabbled around in the semi-darkness, frantic, looking here and there.

A bottle-opener, a corkscrew; Atalanta swung here and there like a puppet with a few of her strings cut.

And the music of Handel rose and fell over both of us like hope or despair.

I donned my periwig. Handel, growing old, heard his music being played by groups of musicians who had long-since lost the precious necessary sympathy. Too fast they played, each violinist competing with the other to finish first! Wondering if, when he talked to himself, people would notice. New age, new tastes, less music.

I straightened the wig, saw Atalanta in the broken darkness struggle to pull the cork out of the bottle, the bottle jammed into the thick folds of the skirt between her legs. Had her mystery come to this? I went over to her, offered my assistance. 'Sit down,' she said, 'sit down and enjoy yourself.'

It was a plea of some sort. I found my armchair and sat back in it, heard the wet plop as the cork slid out, then the metallic rattle as the corkscrew bounced into a dark corner.

The glorious song ended. Atalanta allowed the needle to scratch-scratch its way to the centre of the record. She kneeled in front of me, sending up wafts of funereal mothballish perfume, brandy-and-wine fumes, her eyes glistening, the smile coming and going now. 'Is that my mother's voice, or the voice of someone else? Is it possible to know? How much of our lives do we make up, eh? Maybe this is all a dream – have you thought of *that*?'

'Yes,' I told her. I'd thought of that. I'd thought that it might all be a dream.

'Oh, you're frightened, being here,' Atalanta said; she finished off the brandy in her glass, adjusted herself on her feet, let one hand rest gently on my knee. 'There is no need to be frightened. There is nothing to be afraid of.'

I said nothing. I feared the shadows on the walls, the presence of her beauty and what I took to be her pain. I feared her being so drunk and was terrified by my own hovering drunkenness. I feared that beyond the windows behind me, beyond our front door, there was no world anymore but merely an intense blackness pricked by occasional stars. Were I to scamper out the front door or through the windows, I would fall, fall endlessly, into a bottomless dumb void.

Now and then I was reassured by the faint smell of evening grass melting in from beyond the windows; but I just could not be sure of anything anymore. And I could mention none of this to Atalanta. I was more afraid that she would abandon me, send me home, reject me, than I was of anything else.

Abruptly, laughing, Atalanta stood up. The absence of the pressure of her hand on my knee startled me. A cold patch spread there. She danced back into the shadows, turned the record over, waited until the harpsichords and violins took over, began conducting the music in the yellowing dark. She was whistling. Shrill, out of tune.

Her free hand fluttered like a frantic leaf trying to free itself from a breeze and fall to earth. In her other hand the empty brandy glass glittered like a transparent tennis ball. Would I wish to take her in my arms, the fluttering leaf she had become? Was she the same woman who had enchanted me, or some other, conjured thing?

She moved, danced, gyrated, to the sound of violins and the patient harpsichord and the immaculate diction of the singer. *He was despiséd*, sang Atalanta; *despiséd and rejected*. A man of sorrows.

She spun once, twice around. There was something

blasphemous in her witchy dancing, a hint of mockery. The music was solemn, respectful; Atalanta manipulated it, made it into something she could dance to, long whirling circles, a grotesque ballet. Her wig flared out with her skirt; the necklace jewels, real or paste, caught fire in the candle-glow. And without any warning she grabbed the bottle of wine and ran out of the room, jerking the door open viciously. For a moment, half-glad to be alone, I relaxed and listened to the music.

Handel, old, working day and night, his housekeeper bringing food and drink. No lauding world left anymore, Italian opera dead on its feet. God came into it. God the Restorer of the Spirit. He wept. Scribbling in those words, He was despiséd and rejected of men. Handel wept. Tired, nervous, feeling his age. Feeling rejected. Three weeks, was all, and it was done. Jennens, comfortable in his country squiredom, opinionated, Handel's junior by almost fifteen years, tut-tutted when he heard the final composition. Not as good as he might have done it, said the librettist. Over unwarm chocolate in the morning Handel reviewed his manuscripts. His Spirit was Restored. What matter the length of one's wig?

The almost empty brandy glass sat somewhere at my feet. Drowsiness snuffed out creeping feelings of guilt and shame. I would not feel uncomfortable. Too much of me felt that I had betrayed some kind of moral code instilled by my upbringing: I should not be here, should not be drinking at all, should not, should not. A vision of my mother, open-mouthed in her tiny decay-filled room, breathing her way to death, measuring out the beats, no longer part of the world she had worried in for so long. Should I be with her? Night and day, dutifully? Or should I do what I was doing, remote, detached, playing in a world so alien to her she could never conceive of it? Was there really a right and wrong in everything?

Questions: I felt my head tilt and the periwig slipped forward. What would my mother say if she could see me now, brought low, cast so far outside myself as I was? Was there room for me anymore in her understanding?

I nodded into that territory between sleeping and waking. Here faces and voices and music converged, merged, became one sound, one idea. My mother's face gave way to images of harvesters in empty fields; half-formed words floated like ragged flags. I tried to stop them as they went by, grasp their meaning. Agnes' face then, laughing; Smithy, huddled and serious, a dour frog. Atalanta, flying by with wings of pink silver. A lake, shimmering in the moonlight, deep and oily; I fell headlong into it, couldn't save myself, started to drown and was grateful.

I woke up with a start, feeling cold despite the shimmering wall of candle-heat around me. The big windows were open, the lake was silent and black, a gentle breeze passed through the room and the bright yellow tongues at the ends of the candles waved and licked the air. No music now, the record had stopped. I felt thick-headed, still drowsy. I sat up on the armchair, my mouth sticky and a horrible taste in it. I wanted more than anything else to sleep beneath warm enfolding blankets, to slip slowly and cosily into my own bed.

The candles had burned down considerably, but, apart from knowing that it was night, I had no concept of passing time. The door to the hallway was open and instinctively I stood up and went towards it.

As I stood up, my periwig fell finally off my head and eased itself down to the floor like a wingless gull, white and helpless.

Twenty-Eight

I stood at the dark mouth of the staircase. I could not believe in the absolute reality of anything now. My legs turned me towards the door and my eyes ached to make me look up; in the dark, the tapestry glowed and the hunters moved, slowly, the unicorn prancing back on its tiny hind legs. I was no longer in control of my movements, the tension in my legs decreased, faded out. There was no fear, just an overpowering curiosity. Besides, I believed I knew where I'd find Atalanta. I moved up the stairs.

Halfway up, drunken giddiness made me think I would overbalance and fall backwards down the stairs. There was the feeling of having climbed a great distance already. I turned past the tapestry and thought I heard the faint distant shout of men on horseback, the croon of hunting dogs. I could have closed my eyes and felt myself becoming enclosed in the hunting scene. Anything was possible.

Then there was the odour of melting wax. It drifted down the corridor from the direction of Atalanta's shattered bedroom. Through the darkness of the unlit corridor a faint yellowish glow intruded. No sound; as I went nearer, the faint murmur of whispered words, a stray giggle, a line of hummed music.

Opening the door of Atalanta's room, I knew, would be entering even further her constantly invented world. Or was I helping her to invent it? By now she was so much a product of my imagination that I suspected I only had to *think* of what she might be up to and she would surely be doing it. It had been necessary for her to play Handel's music and attempt to ape something of the dress and atmosphere of a stuffy concert-hall or drawing-room of his day. It had been further necessary to include me, not just an innocent spectator, but as a conspirator in her fantastical masquerade. Atalanta needed an audience, even a drunken audience of one. I could not imagine loneliness so intense and deep as that. Perhaps I was writing the story of Atalanta, the fiction that was her, step by step? In some way, perhaps, she had made me her biographer. The sense of my being called to witness was strong and carried oddly religious connotations. And I was uncomfortable with it.

I pushed open the door. Candles, everywhere, shadowing the wreckage that had once been a comfortable and probably comforting bedroom. The bed itself seemed to sag in the middle and its wooden frame leaned preciously.

Atalanta sat on the floor in a circle of tall white candles. I imagined a frenzied shopping-trip, the car laden with boxes of candles, everything in slow and deliberate preparation. I thought of this, of the absurdity of it, and felt slightly cheated. So much advance preparation. Like being given a surprise birthday party, halfway through which you accidentally stumble upon all the receipts for the presents, the cake, the cards; mundane, disappointing secrets.

I rubbed my eyes, aware that I had felt almost constant drumming fatigue for hours. Atalanta was obscured by shimmering light, her skirt spread around her. Was she aware of the possible danger of it catching fire? She didn't appear to be; yet at the back of my mind I felt, perhaps unfairly, that all this too had been carefully rehearsed.

She looked up. The manic smile again. The room was stiflingly hot, every breath contained the odour of hot melted wax. Everything seemed in danger of exploding into flame. The intense and vibrant luminosity of the circle in which Atalanta sat was blinding.

I put one hand over my eyes, stood in the doorway, heard the soft lulling monotone.

'Once upon a time,' Atalanta said without looking up, 'I found a ticket to the theatre in a secondhand book. It was in perfect condition. The theatre was in Athens, a play by Euripides. I have never been to Athens. I kept that ticket for a long time and often I would stare at it, concentrate very hard, close my eyes, try to imagine the person who had purchased it; what he or she looked like, what else they did that day, where they lived, their feelings on not remembering where they'd put the ticket. I tried to imagine, holding the ticket in my fingers, the lives led by the person who had bought it. Then one day I closed my eyes and saw the face of a young woman, a woman like myself, darker. Just for an instant, nothing more than an image. All around her the sun shone on the street. That was all. I knew the ticket had not mattered much to her. An afterthought. There was no one else involved. No lover. No mystery. Nothing. And yet the ticket in that book was the key to another life. And it still contained a tiny essence of that life in its paper. Can you believe that?'

As she spoke Atalanta went through the motions of plucking a chicken; she had something in her hand from which she plucked and pulled and vague shreds and bits fled through the flamey atmosphere and scuttled along the floor.

'A girl looking at me on a hot street somewhere in Greece, maybe even in Athens itself,' she said. 'Or maybe not looking at me, maybe looking at the ticket in her hand. The ticket was a window through which I watched her, a window into the past. Can you believe that? I can. And I believe it must be all the more true of our photographs.'

Photographs. Vague figures boarding trains under a hot sun. Women in big hats, enigmatic smiles, beside men in baggy trousers and Brylcreemed hair parted in the dead-centre of the head. Windows. To look at the photos was to watch them, spy on them, see them as they looked before time and death waved a wand over them, introduced something that would not register on a photographic plate. Or *should* not.

I remembered the photographs. It all seemed a long time ago. I remembered them. Atalanta sat in the circle of candles and tore up, one by one, an entire stack of photographs, too bored with their contents to bother looking at them as she did so, tossing their fragments into the air with childish impatience.

I remembered the photographs under decomposing bits of this and that in my own back yard. Private histories made public in a moment of bravado. Lives gone stale pictured at their tremulous height, when all was energy. People I probably knew, passed on the street every day, made tea for in the quiet mornings: but I could no longer recognise them, they did not in the least way resemble the inhabitants of the photographs. They would never resemble them ever again.

Atalanta's photographs – were they any different from mine? – fluttered in pieces over the candles. She watched me, I felt her eyes burning the side of my face. I stopped before the flaming circle – what was it meant to keep out? – and stooped down, picked up a torn triangle of glossy paper. A leg. A segment of naked leg. I stooped again, playing at jigsaw. Slowly I pieced together the form of a naked body, legs splayed lewdly apart. I knew before I found it whose head would be on it. And still the smile. Naked. Her legs not merely splayed but the feet straining outwards, as if she could not open wide enough the angle of her thighs. I recognised the bed she sat against. Bits and pieces of torn torso, arms, legs, head, fluttered out of Atalanta's fingers into the hot air.

Men, now. Or one man in particular. Smiling. Handsome. Naked. Playful. Nothing moved in any of the photographs. Nothing obviously physical, or even sexual. Posed. They were all deliberately posed, held, positioned for the camera. But who, I wondered was *behind* the camera?

Atalanta continued to pluck the pile of photographs and the mad massacre continued to spread itself over the floor.

'To look at the photograph and *feel* the lives being lived within it,' said Atalanta. 'And sometimes you'll know the people there and sometimes you won't. Sometimes you will see them again and sometimes you won't.'

She stood up, the sweep of her skirt almost glancing the rim of the burning circle. She lifted the skirt and stepped over the candles on tip-toe. I found it hard to think she had drunk so much. As she came closer I could smell the drink on her breath, a sickly heavy vapour. She held a photograph face-out towards me. 'See,' she said, 'this is you, is it not? There. In the middle. Isn't it like you? I recognised you in the church at once. It must be you. The likeness is remarkable.'

Frightened, moth-like in my curiosity, I took the old photograph from her hands. Trapped in the isolation of whatever world McKinley had dragged her to, Atalanta had invented whole lives and histories from photographs. Yes, I suppose it might have been me: in a Victorian sailor-suit, standing beside a little girl who bore no resemblance whatever to Atalanta, posing beside two towering adults, stiff, without smiles, ruffles and neck-brooch and immaculately pressed trousers and fob-watch, against the typical studio backdrop of the day. A studio in Belfast, the gold script-lettering decorated the bottom of the card into which the photograph was pasted. The photograph was surprisingly clear, every detail on the figures was sharp.

The little boy looked like me and did not look like me, as the flickering candlelight played with his image. At least eighty years old. At least.

'My favourite,' Atalanta said. 'When I would look at this photograph, the hours wouldn't seem so long. I imagined great things for the little boy and the little girl. I gave them names. He is Tom and she is Matilda. They were my friends. They stayed with me when I was alone. I gave them lives, places to go, things to do. And I made them grow up. I was their mother and father and big sister. I *made* them.'

Then she tore the photograph out of my hand and ripped it up as she had done with the rest. I imagined Tom and Matilda screaming somewhere, even under the ground. Who, I wondered, had invented the naked girl, the naked Atalanta, in the other photographs? Loneliness was everywhere in that destroyed, candlefogged room. It had its own smell: burning and mothballs. So, Atalanta was inventing me too. From what she had already invented from a photograph of people most likely dead. A story being written. A novel that began on its final page and went forward to the first. A feeling of not being substantial, of not being quite connected to my own body, slithered over me. I felt that, with a flick of her fingers, Atalanta might tear me up too.

Twenty-Nine

Atalanta stood directly in front of me, the glowing circle of candles providing a halo for her absurd and somehow indecent wig.

All the myriad smells of the room, and then, over them, Atalanta's alcoholised breath: sweet, foetid, decaying.

I saw that she wore a thin veil of powdery white make-up which had cracked around her eyes and at the edges of her mouth, little rivers of refusal, inlets of age. Her eyes were wide and wet, as if she had been asleep. They seemed to darken as she drew me into them.

Age would not be kind to her; her beauty was meticulously flawed, peeling away with infinite patience. I thought of Agnes, of what she had been like to my childish eyes when I'd struggled to write a whole play about her; a beauty distilled from my own affections, blinded by an unknowing and uninformed love.

And what she was like now, almost a mother yet still a playful child, her beauty blown apart by a thousand bodily changes she had no say over, weighed down by the splitting of cell upon cell, the alchemy of mindless regeneration. No, it wasn't Smithy's fault: it was the fault of something much greater, a vast and disinterested Nature. The cruelty of it was enormous and blind; Agnes would fall under its hand, as Atalanta was beginning to. There was no appeal, no remission.

Atalanta smiled her smile again and I pictured my mother, the face of dozens of family photographs, a good-looking woman by all accounts, tumbling downwards into decay in an overheated and darkened room where no visitor stayed for long. For some odd reason I felt compelled to touch my cheek with my fingers. Soft skin still. A nurtured growth of harmless stubble. Here and there a soft eruption of acne.

Atalanta replaced my fingers with her own, lightly brushed my skin with their tips, up and down, looking into my hair, my eyes, so close that I could see minute flakes of make-up detaching themselves and whispering into the hot air. I found it difficult to breathe. I was no longer sleepy but floating between the floor and the tips of Atalanta's fingers in a kind of numbed hypnosis.

'So easy,' Atalanta said, 'so easy, so easy. Innocence cannot be replaced. You are a virgin in the world. *Yes. Yes.*'

There was a beat, a rhythm to her words. This was more than language.

Again, a spurt of fear trickled across my abdomen. The touch of her fingers was deceptively soothing and reassuring. I felt my feet find the floor again. I began to relax. Her fingers trickled down my cheek and throat. I stared into her deep black eyes, feeling her body edge closer, the ruffles and frills and enormities of the skirt peeling back as she angled herself forward. I felt her body arch into mine. Blood rushed to my face. I could not look at her now, the thick heavy erection in my jeans made me feel powerful and ashamed. I did not know what to do. I felt her breath and the tips of her fingers edge along the dry lines of my lips.

'We are alone in the world,' Atalanta sang, 'we are alone,

there is no one but us. No one but us. Outside there is nothing. This is our world. *This.*'

I turned my face away. In and instant Atalanta angled her body back into the room as if trying to reach something. Then she was pressing against me again. Her face came closer to mine. I felt the hot tangy stickiness of her mouth against the side of my face.

In the background – outside the house, somewhere in the dangerous dark of the real world – something fell. A dull uninteresting thud, as if a large book had been dropped on the floor, or a heavy sack had tumbled off the back of a truck. I took no notice of it. It seemed to be far off. Nothing out there was of any consequence. Perhaps Atalanta was right; perhaps there was nothing in the whole world but us. I felt her mouth against my cheek again, and slowly turned my face to meet it.

Surprised, Atalanta stepped back. Hair had fallen over her face, she looked like a doll that has been shaken violently.

She closed her eyes and I brought my mouth – my own eyes wide open – against hers, my dryness against her wetness, a crude, tentative, probing, without any particular sensation of pleasure. Then she placed her arms around my neck, pulled me into her, her mouth opening now, wide and swallowing, her tacky saliva full of stale alcohol. She opened her mouth painfully over mine, I couldn't breathe, I pulled back, pressed my hands against her shoulders, felt the odd pressure of something sharp and solid against my neck; then she released me, stood back, a destroyed, half-made-up face and her wet mouth dangling open.

It was all madness now. She brought one hand up quickly and I saw the camera, saw her steady herself to focus it, and turned my face away just as the flash went off. I ran out of that room, hearing her coming after me, hearing her voice rise and fall behind me as she chased me as far as the top of the stairway.

'Come back!' she said, 'please, please come back! We are history now!'

I ran down the dark stairs, hardly caring if I tripped and fell.

'I'm sorry,' Atalanta screamed: harsh, shrill, like the distressed cry of a wounded bird. 'I'm sorry: forgive me, *forgive me!*'

A sound that carried like the screech of a peacock.

But I kept going, afraid, saddened, confused. I could no longer understand anything, interpret anything. I no longer possessed the strength. It was all a dream; a dream, or the most seductive madness. The spotted blindness of the flashlight stayed with me, a blue explosion in my eyes. I felt the hardness of the hallway floor under my feet and slowed down.

Looking back up the stairway I saw the shadowed figure of Atalanta in wig and wide skirt, the camera dangling in one hand, silent, unmoving, watching me, as if she were under a spell which did not permit her to move down the stairs. Behind her the tapestry twitched mockingly. '*Please,*' she said; a word breathed so softly now that I could barely hear it. I turned, pulled at the handle of the big front door, and went out into the night.

A chill breeze slapped my face. I breathed deeply, then retched vigorously into the dark. The fumes of brandy, wine and half-digested food rose up like a poisonous gas, but I felt better. My heart slowed down. I began walking, knowing somehow that Atalanta would not follow me, and that I would not go back if she sent for me. There was too much Smithy in me, too much Agnes. Something like that. I just felt happy and relieved to be out of the house.

When I reached the main road I could see a warm pulsating glow in the sky, a biblical light, over the trees, the sleeping fields, over the big machines tucked away for the night.

The first houses were coming near, and my own house was in darkness, and I stepped aside to allow an ambulance to pass on the unlit road, a white blur, whipping up the breeze, a blue light flashing and its whine breaking the dark silence into fragments. I filled my mouth with saliva and spat into the black hedges. The air was sweet with cut grasses and a light frost, and the sickle moon had risen and turned slightly. I heard men's voices in the distance and the growl of heavy engines.

Thirty

My father's blow was short and sudden. It took me across one side of my face, reddening my cheek, making it burn.

Ernest May's public house was now a gaping, burning, smoking hole in the square, like the remains of a rotting tooth ripped from a jaw. The Unknown Soldier did not move, not a muscle.

'I know where you've been,' my father said, staring at me, angrier than I'd ever known him to be.

The sound of water under great pressure sizzled and hissed in the air.

'The woman's a slut,' my father said, spitting into my face. 'Drink on ye, into the bargain.'

The smell of burning timber hung in the air: people moved about, stepping on the broken glass, making little explosions under their feet. Police erected a hasty cordon of rope, firemen climbed in through what was left of Ernest May's front window, an ambulance slammed open its back doors, and a stretcher was hoisted inside. Some women cried. Men talked in low whispers. Dogs barked, infuriated by human excitement and dismay.

A dartboard lay on its back, a dart stuck on the double-twelve. Bits and pieces of the big brewer's mirror, like an obscene light-filled jigsaw puzzle, lay scattered over the wet roadway. Ernest May and his wife propped themselves up against a wall, dazed-looking, fending off police questions, looking as if they didn't know where they were. There was blood on Ernest May's forehead and an ambulance attendant came over to him and tried to prise his hand off the wall but he wasn't coming.

'If your mother could see ye,' my father said: and then he trailed off into a mumble, looking around him, seeing a brother of his, hailing him, glad to be out of my way and desperately confused in a way that made me pity him. He was out of control. His world had been falling apart. Now someone had blown it up.

Smithy and Agnes moved in and out of the tight gossiping mobs like two lost ghosts.

Agnes was very fat now. She saw me, looked away. Smithy saw me too, raised a limp hand to wave, let it drop, dead. Something much bigger than any of us, any of our petty differences and squabbles, had happened. Ernest May's wife saw her husband being lodged finally in the back of an ambulance and started, alone now, to go hysterical, crying out to be allowed to accompany him. In the end, they loaded her in too.

Fire leapt and spat out of the shattered pub roof. I moved closer, still drunk enough, mesmerised by the destruction. From one madness to another. The world had tilted on its axis. Nothing was safe or certain anymore. Big fishermen tried to pull planks out of the way and scorched their hands. Here and there men sat upon the ground like children, hurt, almost in tears, having a hand bandaged hastily, a cheek daubed. Flashing blue and orange roof-lights made a macabre dancehall out of the square. The fire engine's humming note rang a discord over every other sound.

A sharp crack, and part of the roof came down. Someone said how lucky the Mays were to be down in the cellar tapping barrels when it happened. Nobody dared say or hint at what *it* might have been. People from all over the area, regardless of creed, used May's pub for darts matches, competitions, outings. Whatever was going on in Belfast was remote, miles away, beyond our ken. We took little notice. We were safe, civilised. Headlines, radio reports, were not reality. The screams of Ernest May's wife were, however, a terrifying song for solo voice against the chorus of the roof timbers falling slowly and with great malevolent deliberateness into the shattered pub.

Ernest May's face came into my head. I stared at my hand, at someone else's blood and could not take my eyes away. I felt great powers under my arms, lifting me. I was unsteady on my feet. My father had me now, his brother Isaac to one side.

'Take that scamp home out of that,' his brother said, 'into bed is what he needs.' My father loaded me like a sack of potatoes into his wee van and we drove out of the mess of the square; so much for the protection of the Unknown Soldier.

I was halfway between laughing and crying, between elation and nausea. My father drove in a deep utter silence, the smell of woodsmoke on his clothes and presumably on mine also. I felt something had moved under the very earth itself, threatening, unyielding. A badger's eyes spat red fire back at us, caught for an instant in the weak headlights.

'Say nothing about this to your mother,' my father said suddenly.

I did not know if he meant about my being drunk or the destruction of Ernest May's pub and the giddy feeling that the terror of the rest of the Province had finally, like a creeping disease, touched us. In the car that night, they weighed equally in the scale of things. My father knew I'd been with Atalanta, but he could not have guessed what had passed there, the abyss which had opened, culminating in the destruction in the square. Were they all one thing, the one great summoning up of madness? Was there a dark army on the move, insinuating itself into our minds, making us mad and the victims of madness in others?

My father thought it still important that my dying darkened mother should be protected from it all or even news of it. It didn't seem to make sense to me. Dying, what would another piece of the dark matter? We drove on, midges bouncing and dying against the windscreen, night all around us, over the silent fields, dripping through the trees like thick, black blood.

My father helped me out of my clothes, helped me wash, made sure the blood was scrubbed from my hand – *whose* blood? – and saw me to bed. He'd quietened down. I heard him pace around for a while, then switch on the radio. Late into the night the radio was still on, as if he listened for something of immense importance. At one point he tried the television, but, dissatisfied with that, snapped it off. Perhaps he wanted to know if the rest of the world had been told of the events in the square, thought this village thing important enough to broadcast. At last I heard him moving about in his own room – *their* own room – until a bedspring creak told me he was in bed too. I suspected he stared for a long time at the ceiling. The sound of cars or heavier vehicles scattered past the house for a long time. Gradually, nervously, I drifted off to sleep.

I had an unsettling dream. A face emerging through the water. A man's face in a curled white wig, surfacing. As it broke the skin of the water, the features of the face melted away as the water peeled back from it. In the end, a brief few seconds, there was nothing but a bare and gleaming skull.

I woke up, hearing a faint fading echo of my own scream in the dark room. Sweat saturated the bed and my vest. I put my arms behind my head and relaxed, blinking now and then into the darkness. My window was always left open a little and beyond it the softness of the fields pulsed and palpitated. The smell of dewy grass, the sounds of birds waking up. I got out of bed.

The sickle moon sat silent, lovely, bright, at an angle to the rest of the earth. The sky was luminous with starlight. I could hear the fields and the sky and the stars. I could hear them humming, a light musical note. I leaned out of my window and felt the cool breeze on my hot skin. I closed my eyes, felt the utter trembling luxury of it all. And something else. Something sensuous and seductive.

I thought of Atalanta. I saw her again standing in front of me, gathered the memories of her breath and the touch of her tongue. *Yes, yes.* If only I hadn't been afraid. If only I hadn't been such a boy, more of a man. I could have completed the demolition of my own world. She had said it and it was true. It was so easy. So terrifyingly easy. There was nothing to it. I could have reached forward and taken Atalanta, a widow, years older than me, taken her down on to the scattery ragged floor of the bedroom, raised the clumsy volume of her skirt. So easy.

Yet I had been afraid. My hand was already in my pyjamas now, but nothing stirred. I was too tired, too loosened from my intake of drink. I came in, closed the window but did not lock it, got back into bed and slept without dreaming.

Thirty-One

Johnny Henderson, our postman veteran of the Korean War
who enjoyed rolling an American accent around in his mouth,
was playing darts when he was killed in Ernest May's pub.

All the big newspapers carried his photograph, a scrappy
one, taken years ago, with our Johnny smiling lamely. A
background of open sky and a stark tree. The stripped
iconography of photographs once again.

Anonymous witnesses remembered conflicting things.
People invented their own lurid versions of the truth, granted
themselves importance in front of a TV camera, under the
phallic jab of a microphone. Someone had left a bomb near the
counter. It seemed that Johnny never had as many friends when
he was alive as when he was killed: it seemed as if the whole
country wanted to distance itself from what had happened and
at the same time acknowledge the horror of it.

There was a murmuring deep in the earth, a chant, as if a
great spell against terror and death were being cast. In the small
shops, in M'Whinney's, under the Unknown Soldier, at the bus-

stop, in the bookie's, down on the quays, people talked about nothing else. It was Johnny's death that weighted the whole thing down. From a terrifying incident to an almost inconceivable horror was the step Johnny had taken for us. He had dragged Ardreagh behind him into the rest of Ulster. We were one with those others who had lost people in blasts and bombings. The Unknown Soldier became Johnny Henderson.

News broadcasts carried reports of the explosion, named Johnny. On the TV, there were pictures – taken in the hard sunlight of morning – of the burnt-out hull of May's pub. No-one mentioned the dart-board and the double-twelve. Perhaps I'd imagined it. The TV also carried that smiling photograph of Johnny. He was famous. Ernest May, interviewed, seemed confused and guilty, as if he'd somehow contributed to the incident by virtue of his having been a broadminded, fair, all-embracing person who got on well with everybody, free of bigotry of any kind. It seemed to be a crime to be well-liked and like other people in these days. Fishermen, it seems, cannot easily grant themselves the dubious luxury of bigotry. In a killing sea, a man's religion or political leanings count for nothing. It's all the same in the teeth of a storm when a boat might capsize. They look into the sky and sniff the wind for signs of struggle and turmoil. They do not look for these things in each other's eyes. I had for my part never once heard my father, his brothers, or anyone else in our area speak an unkind word against someone on the grounds of his religion or colour or politics. And we lived comfortably free of suspicion.

The death of Johnny Henderson drove a knife into our community. Its blade was sharp with anger and suspicion. Now weedy silences grew where smiles had once flowered. The big harvesters finished their work in the fields and men sat about under their purring shadows smoking, eating, drinking, in a crazy kind of torpor. For days I did not hear laughter. The smell of cut grass and the scurry of frenzied rats at the side of the road; whatever was natural and expected took on blacker aspects. There were dark omens; one afternoon dead fish were washed into the harbour, scores of them. Two fields away, men cleaning the engine of a harvester found a crow in the funnel, it was still alive. A cormorant, a bird rarely seen in our area, preened itself on the shoulder of the Unknown Soldier and roosted there for three days.

My father slid into an impenetrable silence. For hours he would say nothing, move around me as if I wasn't there. The atmosphere of our house was heavy with what I expected him to say, and still he said nothing. He never referred to Atalanta's house or that he knew I'd been there, ever again. He drove to Belfast to see my mother; now and then I went with him, entering a city obscured as if by a light smog of fear and suspicion.

Passing the pubs after leaving the hospital you could hear barbarous laughter pitted against the blaring interruption of TV sets. Barbed wire, armoured vehicles that moved, big-wheeled, with an insect's slowness, police-stations that cowered behind high walls of tin, cement, wire, and the unblinking eyes of twitching cameras.

On the street corners, boys yelled '*Telly!*', for the *Belfast Telegraph*. The City Hall, sprayed with anxious starlings, sat like an elaborate piece of tableware in its cushion of green, pinpricked by statues. Inside, when I was a child, my father had shown me the Solemn League And Covenant with its signatures in blood.

My mother was conscious at various times now, bald as a tiny newly-hatched bird, fiddling to adjust her wig on her head in case we'd see. She was full of erratic petty demands, irritations that left us both silent and exasperated at the side of the bed. Had I enough to eat? Had I a decent coat now that the weather would be changing? Yes yes yes. Not a word about the bombing of Ernest May's pub and the death of Johnny Henderson, our postman. My father's security system was airtight: there had been no leaks. Nothing of the outer world penetrated very far into the bowels of this humming brownish maze of quietly closing doors and yellow-lit rooms. The dying were irritated by bedsores, cramped muscles and acute spasms of pain, but never by violence in the outside world. The violence taking place in their own bodies was enough.

Sometimes I would play at propping my mother up in heavy thick pillows. The smell of decay in the room, a hot and sweetly-sick smell, never eased. I wondered whether my mother could smell it and recognise it. She was in pain almost constantly and consequently was drugged to one degree or another most of the time. At times her breath went, her eyes would close, and she would seem to struggle with something, fight it off, come back to us shakily, a little weaker. The absurd and sad wig would shift, slide, reminding me shiveringly of other wigs worn at another time in another place. Wigs would not leave me alone. Outside her pale window a decently modest evening light swung up and down the carpark, wearing itself out. The window was of thickly waved and ruffled glass, so even had she possessed the strength to prop herself up, she could not have made out anything through it.

My father attended to her with determined dignity and care: a glass of water, a pill, tissue to wipe her dry mouth, the wig. Did I feel anything? Hardly anything. So used had I become to hopping from one world to another, from one reality to the next, that I easily removed myself from my mother, the dying, the room. I had nothing to say here, nothing to do.

As I said, I made pretence of doing things, determined to appear dutiful and busy. It was a pale effort, made to look good in front of my mother and for my mother's sake. I could not account for the automatic nature of it all, of my breathing, of my steps towards the bed, adjustment of pillows, whatever it was. Sometimes the lack of feeling unnerved me, as must be the case when a man gets his sight back and is flooded with new and unpredictable light. The shock and wonder comes later.

But I stumbled, or began to stumble, more and more about the room, wondering when my father would finally stand up and back towards the door, stifling the thought that he might never see her alive again.

I was already gone. My mother's dying, Ernest May's tragedy, Atalanta herself – all were part of me and were what I was, conclusions and beginnings. I was no longer capable of imagining the rough romantic scribbles of the child who had composed a play about a girl called Agnes. Something inside me had dried up forever.

My mother's hand, light as a feather and transparent as blue glass: out into the quiet hallway smelling of floor-wax, watching the hallway floor shine all the way down its length. Red-wheeled fire hoses on the walls; a cry somewhere far off, the sound of someone whistling. Patience of a kind found nowhere else but in wards like these. Patience that lives in the walls of the house of the dying.

Thirty-Two

My father had ceased his crazed habit of hunting for a doctor and an opinion. Now he closed the door as if it would break.

This evening it was still blue and bright when we got into the car. We drove through easy evening streets, under Union Jack flags hanging out from shops, under the ever-watchful horizontal eye of Napoleon's face up on Cave Hill, taking a peculiarly different route this time, over different bridges, slogans on walls, warehouses, the river Lagan flowing with brown simplicity towards the lough and the Irish Sea. Gantries. My father stopped the van, rolled down his window. The noise of the city, a deep brown baritone, came in.

He looked at me, then looked over the water at the gantries of Harland and Wolff Shipyard, at the single Goliath crane, pompous and dark yellow with the letters H & W on it high up in the clouds, legs splayed contemptuously over its miniature kingdom of iron, steel and water.

My father looked at me and asked me bluntly what I intended to do with myself now that university was out of the question. Shakily, I told him I could always go back and try another year at a Tech' for a couple of more exams.

'You'll not', he said. 'That's a waste of time for a lad like you. There's a streak in you I don't know where you got it. Half the time you're up in the sky somewhere. You have me worried about you.'

The gantries seemed to lean down a little to hear what was going on. In the river air, dirty gulls screamed and circled.

'You need sense put in your head,' my father said. 'You need to get *practical* with yourself. I know what I'm talking about. You need to start earning your keep, get yourself a sense of responsibility.'

He said all this while staring over the water at the shipyard. Then I felt the question growing against my will and I asked him: 'Da, do you ever regret not being a fisherman?' He didn't turn around, kept staring at the water, the gantries. When he replied I could hardly hear him. I couldn't make out what he said.

Silence, then, for a very long time or what seemed like a very long time. I fidgeted, not knowing what to expect next. I wanted to be a writer, I wanted him to know that so that he wouldn't ever ask me again.

'I'm getting you a start in the 'Yard, son, I've been speaking to a man. There's nothing for you round our way but fishin' and I can't see you at that, so there's nothing. And I just don't want you hangin' about one arm long as the other. Signin' the Buroo. You'll start small and work up like many's a man had to do and maybe it'll give you a sense of responsibility. You can always leave if you don't like it.'

My father went on for a long time apologising, saying how if he knew more people he could have fixed me up with a better job but it was a start. Things were changing, he said, and my mother was dying and it was time I stepped into the world. He kept wanting me to *understand*.

In the end the whole thing became a litany and I didn't hear it anymore. My future had hit a brick wall. I was not in control of my own life, it had been folly to imagine I ever had been. Plans were made for me, directions arranged; I was dumb, helpless. Ashamed of myself, I hung my head, twiddled my thumbs; my father's decree had the weight of a punishment.

We drove off. I looked around the city and felt the queer anguish of exile. I hadn't stood up for myself, the *writer*. Needing the right words, I'd stumbled upon my lack of them. Perhaps my father thought I was in some sort of danger at home, left to myself and my imagination. He was doing for me what his instincts dictated and there was nothing the matter with that and yes I knew I could always leave the job if I didn't like it. He would arrange a place to stay. I could come home on days off. It was a start. It was the *start* that was important.

The one person in the world I needed to talk to, to tell, I had sworn to myself not to see again no matter what the reason.

I thought of her face, how we had been that glorious distant day at the beach, and felt hot pangs in the pit of my belly. Regret. Remorse. They sniped at me, took cover, came out again as we drove through the streets under the stare of the gantries. Maybe it's all for the best, I told myself. There are signs that the world is changing, that's true. My fear of Atalanta struggled with a need to sit with her one more time before I entered upon exile.

Night fell slowly as we left the city, past a vast cemetery, past a flock of quiet deep-green hills, through an Army roadblock, towards home.

Thirty-Three

Johnny Henderson had no relatives.

He was buried under the lustful gaze of TV cameras on a hot white afternoon, the hearse and following cars kicking up dust and yellow earth from the roads, scattering the flagrant feeding rats.

The tombstones felt hot under the fingers; crows keened in bare flattened fields. Now and then a faint breeze blew up, cool and mischievous. A few leaves fluttered down from weary trees, brown and curled at the edges. All Ardreagh was there. Not the women, of course, just us men. At the graveside Reverend McAspey, gowns flapping and tugging, intoned *Dust Thou Art* and *In Sure Hope*. He reminded us that the Lord alone had the right of vengeance: *Vengeance is Mine, sayeth the Lord*. Amen, my uncle Isaac answered, choired steadfastly among his brothers. Stiff black coats shielded the open grave. Johnny disappeared into the good harvested earth.

A sullen, thiefy edginess crept over Ardreagh. Nothing that anyone could do, surely, would break the thin tough surface of fear and uncertainty that lay like a frost over all of us. I was to be sent out of it, into a city full of new and similar terrors. My exile was being prepared for with slow deliberateness. My father contacted a relative, an ageing aunt who had married into Belfast and never come out of it. I would stay with her: fusty front rooms, odour of wilting geraniums in big brass pots, thick curtains and purplish 'black-out' blinds still on their wartime rollers; a rail outside the door where, once upon a time, gentlemen and gentlewomen might scrape the street from the soles of their shoes: tea served conscientiously in thin-rimmed cups and thin water-biscuits would come on a thin plate. Red brick, thin bay windows. A toilet in the back yard, coal heaped against a whitewashed wall; a scullery with stone flags, a stone sink, the perpetual smell of cold and soap.

I languished around the roads, the fields, the lanes, soaking up the sun and the smells. Perhaps I would remember where I was going . . . I was like a refugee awaiting documents in a hostile land.

One day a Post Office van, red and small and fast, went by me. A new, younger postman, no more bicycles. The fields burned, turned yellow and brown under the heavy-handed sun. In the evenings a cooling breeze got up again and I donned a thin pullover.

Agnes could barely walk around the square, arm-in-arm with Walter Smith, neither of them acknowledging the rest of the world, steeped in doom. Ernest May's pub was now a boarded-up hole. The injured, released from hospital, stood on corners debating the whole event over and over, scratching the grubby casts on an arm here, a leg there, staring down at where their pub used to be. There were plans being made, tentatively, cautiously, to find a new place to hold darts matches. Double-twelve. The death throw.

Reverend McAspey caught me wandering about the grave-yard one day like a bored ghoul – I was looking for our family plot and I couldn't find it – he called me over. He was dressed out in his visiting suit. He looked athletic and young in it.

'I hear you're going to Belfast on us soon,' he said. He grinned down at me. Behind him, a watery blue sky. The season was on the turn.

Here was the man who had buried McKinley. I looked at him, startled that he knew about the Belfast business, and aware too that my father had discussed it with him. Instinctively, my father would have called on his minister.

'Yes,' I answered, 'I'm going into the shipyard.'

'Well,' said Reverend McAspey in the same tones with which he'd reminded us all of dust and resurrection, 'sometimes in life we have to begin at things that we don't necessarily like. You'll enjoy Belfast after you get used to it.'

'If I don't I'm coming back,' I said.

'Well-well,' said Reverend McAspey.

A small green fly alighted on his stiff grey shoulder, then swooped away. I told him I was looking for the family grave and he pushed me through the acre or so of tombstones and found it, a leaning headstone, broken by weather, roots, years. Our name was still there, fading but readable. And there was room for other names, we had a fair-sized piece of graveyard. We went back a fair bit, too; men, boys, girls, wives. Names like Liza, William, Johnny, Gladys, Edith and a wayward-sounding Polly. Names that would startle no one. My mother's name would be next.

I stood for a moment or two wondering what it was like under the earth; did you know when people came to visit?

Then the Reverend McAspey put me in his car and drove me to his church.

It was cool inside, the regimental commemorative plaques sang brassily in the grey light. Up by the altar, various fruits of the field, vegetables, wheat, barley, some home-made bread, had been laid out, along with a bottle or two of home-made jam and apple juice, a generous heap in thanks for a good year.

Reverend McAspey seemed to relax in his church, happier in God's house than walking His earth. The suit sat comfortably on him in here. We moved across the church, I glanced back at the offerings of the earth; a thin sheaf of barley shifted to one side, staggered like a drunken man, and fell very quietly out of its place on the pile.

There was a small and very old library behind a locked door, I doubt if many people knew it was there. Dust everywhere, playing in the thin squeezed light from a dirty narrow window high in the wall. The books seemed to creak with age, shelved tightly, their thick leather spines protesting. Small and big books, hymnals, Bibles, ledgers. The Reverend McAspey found what he was looking for. A big ledger, lined, opening with a puff of disdain. Thin writing, in ink, black ink, a nib that might have been carved from a goose's feather.

Parish Records, Reverend McAspey explained; though it was obvious enough. Names, dates, sex. Birthdays, deathdays, dates of marriage, Christenings, everything. How many lives were crowded, muttering, into the pages of this ledger? I looked at the names and imagined faces, smiles, grimaces, engaged in everyday war with life, taking happiness as a hostage. The ledger spoke of pain – children dead before they had lived six weeks – and of outbreaks of happiness, several weddings over a period of a few months. Or perhaps they weren't *too* happy, either; I thought of Agnes and Smithy, who, so far, had shown no inclination to enter their names in this book.

I saw a whole world of Ardreagh open up in front of me, the pages spoke to me of the history of a small place and maybe if I listened closely I could hear where this small place was going. But all the songs sung by the clicking pages were of times long passed.

'There you are,' said Reverend McAspey, 'there's your grandfather and your grandmother's wedding, see?'

I leaned over and saw their names and imagined long dresses and stiff collars. A severity locked in ritual and religious observation. Good-living people.

'And there's your Dad's birth, just there.'

There it was. My father, an infant in the hands of people I had never met, they were dead mischievously before I was born. 'Your Granny's favourite song', my father had told me one quiet evening, listening to a piano piece by Chopin: *Deep is the Night,* sung by a woman in the early hours of this century.

'There's your uncles, and your grandfather's death, and then your grandmother's death, and then your dad's marriage.'

The Reverend McAspey went on, and I saw that my mother's middle and never-used name was Francesca, far too elaborate and elegant a name for the wife of a fisherman. But it had a sad wonderful unearthly ring to it. There was my own christening: a lone cry, never again sounded in our house. Why was I alone, left alone? Who would I ask?

The Reverend McAspey turned the pages. Names, dates, blew into the air. My father had been parentless when he had met my mother. Going out to sea and coming in with his brothers starting to marry all around him. There was an echo of a conversation in my head, something overheard, that he'd met her during the Second World War at a dance in Belfast. Black-out streets, bombers over the aircraft factory. St Anne's Cathedral cut in half, they had been rebuilding it ever since. I saw that my father and my mother were both legends, myths, and histories. The outlines of novels came up at me from the ledger. Stories to be told, secrets to be unravelled.

And Reverend McAspey came to the ornate and carefully-scripted entries of the McKinley family.

As soon as I saw the name a vague music started up in my head, or was it in the room? The image of the falling sheaf of barley drifted back to me, I heard a door open in the church. For some reason, or perhaps none, the minister hesitated before the entries; they went back a very long way. He seemed to run his eyes over them, seeking something, a frown on his face. For the moment he seemed to forget about me. Something flapped quickly against the narrow window, a shadow over both of us, the books. He turned a page and there, sure enough, was the death-entry for Reginald McKinley. Before it, the record of his childless marriage to Atalanta. Or rather, to a girl named Marie Atalanta Valle-Dumarc.

Reverend McAspey saw me staring at the name.

'I think she must be French,' he said awkwardly. When Reverend MAspey spoke, a withering poshness oiled every vowel and syllable. He moved his hands lightly, as if afraid to let them rest against anything of this world. 'There, a place given as Mont Saint-Jacques. God knows where it is. I've never heard of it. Have you ever visited France?'

'No,' I said.

'Maybe some day, eh?'

'Yes,' I said. 'Maybe.'

Marie Atalanta Valle-Dumarc: how had she been, what had she been doing, when McKinley first laid eyes on her? Where were her family? Did she mean what she had said about her mother? Marie was such a simple, unsophisticated name for the person Atalanta was. No wonder she'd preferred her second name; I thought of my mother, and how she had kept the beautiful name Francesca out of the vulgar mouths of the world. The Reverend McAspey closed the heavy tome with a soft smack. 'Your Dad seems to think you'll fare well in Belfast, eh? For the time being, at any rate.'

Again the Reverend left me wondering exactly how much had been discussed regarding my future. Had my father mentioned that he suspected I spent time with McKinley's widow? Reverend McAspey ushered me out of the little library and bolted and locked the door behind us. The church seemed quieter than before. At the top, directly opposite the offerings of the harvest, a single figure draped in Victorian black from head to foot slipped in to a pew and knelt down. Then, as if forgetting some propriety or other, the figure came up from kneeling position and sat down on the polished bench, back straight as a rod, unmoving.

Reverend McAspey blinked as we came into the evening sunlight. The fields slept early these days, birds rose and settled on them, a scurrying of rats could still be heard from the road. The smell of the sea, salt and ammonia, drifted over to us on a light breeze.

I was looking around for a certain car, but could see it nowhere. In the days since I had fled her house, I had heard nothing; no Johnny Henderson with a cryptic card in an envelope. The new sleek postal van seemed unfit for such deliveries. Nothing. Not a word. At the gate of the church, our feet on gravel now, the Reverend McAspey put his graceful, Old Testament arm on my shoulders.

'You've a lot to be proud of, son, being born around here. Your family were all good fine Christian people, God-fearing, loving people. You have what a lot of people would give all the money they have to get, a *place* in the world. You know who your people are and by the Grace of the Lord you know who *you* are. Reflect on Joseph in exile from his brothers.'

Never before had it all seemed so important or meant as much as then. I smiled, and I meant it. Reverend McAspey smiled back. 'You probably have no faith in the goodness of the Lord at all,' he said. 'But no man is barren ground, son, and the Spirit of the Lord Jesus Christ springeth like clear water and floweth where it will out of the rock of the Lord.'

I felt solid, standing there. Yes, it was important to have a headstone of your family in the graveyard and your names down in a register in the church. There was nothing old-fashioned or silly about this. There was a sense of flow, of continuity, that was like feeling the blood in your veins. It meant you were alive. I am written, therefore I am. Because the others are inscribed, I *am*. A funny kind of almost religious thing. But somehow very important. Without it, you could simply drift wherever the current took you. Nothing anchored you. You drowned, eventually. Reverend McAspey had thrown in his own message for good measure. On the edge of exile, I was grateful for it.

He asked me to come and see him any time I wanted before I left, and I said goodbye and went off down the road, irritated in my good feelings by the memory of the black-clad figure in his church. Something told me it was, and at the same time was not, Atalanta; perhaps it was Marie? The same person, but different, the difference and weight of difference conveyed by the change of names. When you superimposed one name upon the other, when you replaced Atalanta with Marie, or the other way around, you could *feel* two different people merging and re-emerging from each other.

The breeze blowing in from the sea was cooler now, and when I suddenly stopped and looked up at the road towards the church, it stood bare and outlined dark against the evening sky, the sun doing nothing but helping to shade it, a remote and dishevelled building holding its dignity like an arthritic old woman with a basket of eggs, full of crumbling bones and names in a ledger which, even as I looked back, were fading forever.

Thirty-Four

The year turned its great wheel. Never before had I been so aware of it or felt the changes pulse in my own blood.

There was a slow accumulating descent, a gathering of weight in the air. Birds seemed to circle more slowly, seabirds sat on the bare fields and preened themselves without enthusiasm. The sun still shone with protesting vigour. But now and then, in the early morning, a veil of white mist grew up out of the fields and diluted the sunshine for a few hours.

The school buses passed again in front of our house, new school terms had begun. Uniforms, red and green, fluttered down the road like blown newspaper, the girls attractive in smart new dresses, white knee-socks, one or two of the lads, the younger ones, sporting skull-caps. It seemed a very long time since I had been initiated into school uniforms. A long time too since Smithy had stolen my black cap with its green badge and flung it over the harbour wall, leaving me daft with trying to explain to my mother. Another world, surely.

Between dreaded visits to the hospital I moved about the house for hours like a man in search of something, reading the book on Handel with increasing irritation, as if whatever I had hoped to find there continued to elude me. Nothing, not a word, not a sign, from Marie Atalanta Valle-Dumarc. I wrote the name, this magically extended name, a dozen times or more on various pages of clean paper, wondering each time if they would reveal something. But they did not. The letters sat stubbornly silent on the white sheets like black birds on a snowy field. It was as if the season for secrets had passed.

Posters advertising local dance-bands and Bingo nights had begun to appear on the hoardings erected where Ernest May's pub used to be. Of course, it was said that he planned to build a pub there again. But so far nothing had been done and Ernest May and his wife moved about the town like cruelly deposed royalty who'd been turned into the street. Respect was paid to them, but in time people began to wonder why: they lost their value, tarnished in the rough air of public disregard. Over everything around that square the Unknown Soldier, alias the heroicly dead Johnny Henderson, leaned and prodded his black bayonet.

The newspapers fidgeted gleefully with photographs of other places that looked like Ernest May's on the night the bomb went off. Then there would be photos, isolated in newsprint columns, smiling in wedding-suits or lounging in cardigans, of men and women who had died somewhere in the city of my approaching exile. It did not encourage me.

A ragged-edged sense of calm and jerky purposefulness settled over the village and the fields. Down by the harbour, on the lolling decks of the fishing-boats, men grumbled about other things and discussed older, more comforting fears. Now and then I journeyed to the quayside just to look at something different. I watched the older men knit and mend the nets and listened to the shouts and calls of their sons and sons-in-law, browny coloured small men in thickly knit pullovers, moving among the oily coils of rope and the fish-boxes marked

Ardreagh Fishing Co-operative and the mysterious paraphernalia of fishing-boats. Occasionally, of course, the visits recalled the eaten face of the girl taken from the sea and I had to retreat back up the streets to the square – where the absence of Ernest May's pub stared at me and leered in its turn.

One day, sitting under the Unknown Soldier and playing with a stray black-and-white dog, feeling my own uselessness in the lazy hours of a sun-worn afternoon, I noticed another of what I had come to recognise as omens.

A young woman pushed a pram out the door of M'Whinney's shop and there was a sudden explosion over the rooftops. I looked up.

A giant swan, bewildered and alarmed, flew over the roofs and dropped suddenly, lighting on the raised canopy of the pram. Its weight tipped the pram out of the hands of the young woman, who screamed. The swan flapped loudly on top of the pram; the child wailed, the woman screamed more shrilly; suddenly it rose with a sharp cracking sound into the air and gained height enough to disappear over the buildings around the square. A small crowd calmed the young woman. The child stopped wailing. Peace settled. But something had happened.

Time ticked away like a bomb. Sometimes in the mornings my head would feel packed tight with wool. I watched my father load his wee egg van wordlessly. Then he'd drive off on his rounds. I would now and then buy a newspaper and try to read it. It would tell me very little that I wanted to know. There were occasions of joyless masturbation, deafened by the utter silence of the house, squeezing my imagination like a lemon, trying to conjure up and hold some vague erotic image. They concluded with the familiar descent into heat and sweat and emptiness and sticky shame. Sometimes masturbating was the only thing I had to look forward to in the whole day. I read, masturbated, walked. I had no purpose in the world. My future was decided for me, I hadn't got the courage or wherewithal to run away by myself, I had no holy Ladies to write plays about.

And I could not write, me, who told everybody, and himself, that he wanted to be a writer. No. Nothing would come, nothing would move my pen, my fingers closed only around the illiterate shaft of my penis. My energies seemed to be gradually dissipating. Sucked away by the very air I moved through. At night sleep took its time coming; there was the hand on the crotch again, and afterwards, eyes thickened with false sleep and the distant peeping of insomniac birds.

I could hear my father grumble or call out in his sleep in the next room, a soft abrupt eruption of sound in the black silence that so resembled, on certain nights, death, or at the very least a deep black sleep. A vehicle would slither down the road, going or coming in the wee hours. The world would hesitate: nothing. Now and then a heavier engine sound told me that a grey-painted Land Rover, prickly with police with snubby rifles, was patrolling its solitary suspicious territories, out of its depth in the country roads, insecure without the terror of redbricked terraces and dozing suburbs. The patrol was one of the privileges, along with brief media attention, the bombing of Ernest May's pub had bestowed upon our community.

Sleep would come, full of dreams. Images, contorted faces, snaps of incredible conversations full of meaning yet indecipherable, crept with dull force into my head. Sometimes I would wake up in time to see the door of my room close over quietly, or hear a soft sniggering by the window, the final bars of an incredibly beautiful piece of music dissolve into the ceiling above my head. Tired-eyed, nervous, I would lie in bed in the morning until my father had made a breakfast of sorts, a dead man's breakfast; then I would hear the van go off, get out of bed, inspect my acne, stubble, stare at myself for a long time in the bathroom mirror.

Images and voices and snips of music would fold all around me for a long time until a sturdy consciousness took command. Then I was propelled with a great belling of nerves and adrenalin into awareness of sorts. Sometimes, if I was particularly sluggish, I would find my mind and concentration fixing on some absurd thing, such as a jar of formalined pig's eyes I'd seen once in a biology class. They would stare out of my fixed imagination with the intensity of light-bulbs in a dark room meaning nothing, indicating nothing – dead and ridiculous.

I began to read cereal boxes, their hopeless advertisements and free gift offers: a model airplane, free with every twenty packet-tops, this sort of thing. I collected little black men from marmalade jars, dozens of them, all members of the same crazy orchestra, baton-twirlers, drummers, trombone-players, tuba-players. I took a plastic boat out into the back yard and set fire to it, watching its turrets and bridge melt into one black foul-smelling plastic mess.

One day I walked over a field where barley had once stood as high as my waist and, bending down, picked up a piece of a porcelain or clay jar with the blue-painted word *Cygnus* on it under the image, fading now, of a swan in flight. I found puffballs and kicked them until the air was filled with dust-light spores and my shoes were greyish white. I walked alone among trees and discovered that they spoke to one another. I came home one evening, hungry, refused to eat for no reason I could think of, went out again. My father did not protest. Strength seemed to have dried up in him too. His brothers called from time to time; no longer was I asked to football-matches.

I bought a small tin of beans in M'Whinney's, walked off into an empty field, opened it with a nail, cut myself, threw it away, beans spraying out everywhere. Sauce and blood. I watched the little Post Office van every day; nothing. Dreading her call, I longed for it more than I longed for food or sleep. Something was going away from me and I wanted it back. Days passed into each other, a slow mass of creeping time, syrupy, sweet. Nothing. Not a card. Not a glimpse in the square, on the roads. Her car was absent from the twisty roads of Ardreagh. Marie Atalanta Valle-Dumarc. A name conjured, made-up, from a book of fairy-stories.

And I remembered vividly her tumbling from beauty into masquerade, from some high grace to the rough earth of absurdity. And my part in it, for had I not been her accomplice? Was I not, in some way, responsible? Had I not been a witness, would the charade have taken place at all? Had it not been for my benefit? Gradually the notion that I had in some way been *responsible* for Atalanta's actions on that last night, for her fall from dignity into a very special form of lunacy – a lunacy that I could still love – began to take hold.

It haunted me, already haunted by forms and noises, and began to fill my waking hours. I felt so cut off from the rest of the world that it would have been no surprise to me if I'd reached out my hand towards, say, the wall, and found a thin plate of glass between me and it. I wondered that people could see me, that I hadn't turned invisible. I felt invisible. I felt *not there*.

And the idea that I owed something to Atalanta became my sole justification for opening my eyes every morning.

Thirty-Five

Teufel!

Darkness bothered him. Although the ordinary comforting sounds of carpenters at work could be heard in the distance, the candlelit stuffiness of the room enhanced shadows and moving shapes in corners, and he did not like it. It reminded him of his father's rooms and Giebichenstein: a barber-surgeon's rooms, smelling highly of alcohol. Then there was the Forbidden Room; of course, he'd peeked. The images remained to haunt him. Things in glass jars, eyes . . .

Bock-bocka-bock *went the distant carpenters. In his child's imagination he had seen those forbidden things move, try to climb out. Now, in the same enclosed darkness, he fidgeted. At his age, at fifty-one, amorous pranks were not the thing. Agues visited him. He tapped with a gentleman's stick on the floor. At last a rustling announced visitors. Or one visitor. She stood in the bizarre cast shadows of the half-opened doorway. That women should seek audiences had been nothing surprising in his youth. Now it unnerved him. He did not know why. He rose. The gilded knob of his stick felt cold in his fingers.*

She backed into even deeper darkness as he threw open the door. He had too much to do, this was all too tiring and juvenile.

'Madam,' he said, feeling fatigue give weight to his Teutonic accents, 'Madam, I have no such time for this joke. If you insist on seeing the preparations . . .'

'I would be honoured, Herr Handel.'

He straightened up. She was young. Every woman was, these days. The voice, a trace of something; but he straightened up. She wore a veil, uncommon in England as a point of fashion. Perhaps she was in mourning. Perhaps she was in masque? In any case, she went before him, leading him, making him feel mocked, old.

He hastened to walk beside her. He managed it, the stick tapping ungraciously; he imagined himself as a blind man being led by a stranger's voice.

Suddenly they emerged into the light, Handel saw that she was dressed from head to toe in black, utter black. Her face might also have been black, so completely did the veil cover it. Really! Mysteries irritated him now. There were people he would see to make absolutely sure that no such silly and time-consuming assignations were ever arranged again! Currying favour with the Prince of Wales was no idle task. Politics. Was life a game?

Setting poetry was not easy, and it had tired him; now in honour of the marriage of the Prince to the Princess of Sachsen-Gotha, he had worked day and night to reproduce an ode as an opera. It worked, but only just. There was something menial and unworthy in it all, no matter how you looked at it. In any case, Covent Garden looked like a battlefield, a city sacked. There was too much to do, and the stage-builders were idiots. But a musician in royal favour would receive fawning criticism; few who attended such gatherings knew much about music. He swore at the builders, but the more he swore the more he lapsed into German and they sniggered at him.

He tried to take her elbow, but she pivoted away nicely. He scraped the floor of the stage with the point of his stick; bock-bocka-bock went the comforting mocking carpenters.

In front of them stretched an artificial avenue leading to a temple to the Goddess Hymen. On top of the arch minor gods and goddesses pranced and leered. Around them, balanced with frightening ingenuity, three carpenters like besmocked angels *hovered and hammered and dropped things. Handel raised his eyes to them. A Triumphal Arch came next, more carpenters, and coats-of-arms of the royal personages.*

Handel raised his stick and pointed out these things, watching her from the side of his vision.

Beneath the Arch, Fame trundled about on a cloud singing the royal praises. In letters you could see through, the names of Fredericus and Augusta rode imperiously above. Handel pointed this out too, outlining the opera, the possible but cautious use of fireworks, a grand chorus. He said unguardedly that he hoped for revivals: did she understand that two schools of thought occupied the musical stage in England? They were at war with each other. Why was he explaining this to her? That Irish clergyman Swift had encouraged the writing of Mr Gay's opera – he gave the word a sneer – was she aware of that? Of beggars and barrow-boys! A driveller, to be sure.

Peculiar, how clergymen tended to get involved in politics; even musicians played at it – did she know that? People did not want to listen to the Italian opera any more. It was sacrilege. Turning their backs on a thing of impeccable beauty, an art born in the throats of angels! To laugh like monkeys at Mr Gay's gutter-music!

He'd allowed his face to flush, and he felt ridiculous. He would never have thought himself a bitter man. His Royal Academy – an appointed Director, but he had never been able to think of it as anything other than his – had stumbled and faltered too long, unsure of its aims even when they were spelled out: the preservation and enhancement of the Italian opera. Which was the true opera, sung in the truest musical language. Yet such arguments sounded trite and insubstantial when flung against the tempest of common taste. There was only so much he could do himself, while sensing opinion turn against him; needing supporters, he had few. This is a new age, he was often told; he didn't have far to look to see that, even though he was never quite certain what the phrase meant in terms of himself. In the coffee houses, in Bowes, his favourite, voices were lowered these days when he appeared. Embarrassment. Of course, the Italian opera was supreme, there was no question . . . And his Academy had argued and guffawed too long. No solidarity. And permitted the 'Mr Gay's' of this world to flourish. After Gay would tramp dozens more, offering commonness to commonness.

What would happen to him, the maestro? He feared old age, its uselessness. He had seen others constrict and wither from neglect, the soul drying up. Would Gay make a beggar of him? He feared not being able to rise out of the flames.

She looked at him, while above her head arches rose and deities romped scandalously. Georg Fridiric wanted to hold her, an absurd desire, an embarrassing one, certainly. It passed. He was overcome by a degrading sense of his jowels, the etched rings about his eyes, the tightness of his wrapped collar. He heard the voice of a tired old man, though he was not an old man, reciting a litany of perceived abuses and degrading spites.

And all the time this war of language and of patronage and of who liked what eroded the pure nature of music, degraded musicians, yet it stubbornly refused not to be waged, he could go on . . .

She walked ahead of him and slightly to his right. He looked at her back. Who was she? He could not determine whether she had listened to one word.

'I will never know Parson Swift's motives,' Handel said, lost now in a breathless exuberance of explanations: 'I will hope maybe to visit his country one day. Then I may know more. Satire is a cheap weapon, Madam. I have had to endure its effects. Do you know how much I have in the bank?'

She turned to him. Did she smile behind that veil?

'Herr Handel, I have no wish to know.'

He grunted. She had stopped him. He gathered himself; he had not realised he was so lonely. And loneliness contributed to his anger. There were some who muttered – he heard everything anyone said about him behind his back, there were always gloating messengers – that they would not have him to dine these days, he could rise to such sailorish language. Resentment at the best table gave the meat a rancid flavour.

He stared up at the Triumphal Arch and wondered whether she knew much about South Sea Annuities. His mad dealings, buying and selling.

'All my life I have had to be a businessman,' he said vaguely; as much to explain his own thoughts to himself as to encourage a response from her.

'I have seen Mr Gay's work,' she said. 'I have thought it amusing.'

'It is not opera, Madam. It is a thing of the street! A vulgar thing. But he himself is an admirable man and I have supped with him and spent some pleasant time with him. I can say no more on the matter. I do not begrudge him his sixty-three nights at Lincoln's Inn Fields.'

'And I have seen your Agrippina, that memorably cold winter in Venice. You will recall, Herr Handel? Part of the city froze over? Margherita singing the lead role, surely you recall?'

Handel looked at her, amazed, tried to see through her veil. Could the woman be that age? Almost my own age? It was inconceivable. The voice, the posture. The erect, stiff back. He thought of Domenico Scarlatti. He remembered Margherita Durastanti, a child and angel in one. Perhaps this woman toyed with him, and had garnered her information from someone who had been there.

Above them both, clumsy unmusical men shouted for nails and cursed each other; here and there, a snatch of a street-song, a word, a whistled air. Around the labourers, Immortals flew and jeered. Handel thought deeper thoughts, drew up from a dank well old, half-loved images. No: utterly loved images. From them he had flown into the arms of street girls, tavern girls, and Scarlatti had preserved him even then. It was impossible, inconceivable, that this was the same woman. No! He refused to entertain the idea. Yet he longed hungrily to lift her veil.

'You are puzzled, Herr Handel.'

Her voice, accented; he could not place it. French? Maybe. Yet his mind sought other things: he placed her delicately in Italy, in Naples – Donna Laura.

'In God's name, Madam! I was twenty-three at the time.'

Handel blurted it out, it made no sense. He knew she was frowning at him and cringed to think of what she saw in his puffy face.

'I am not Laura,' she said. He had not mentioned the decaying name, not out loud, yet she knew it.

'There was one other. For whom you composed in French. A cantata? A sweet melodious little thing. Do you remember?'

Handel, dumbfounded, stared. All he saw was a face swathed in black, as his memory became saturated by darkness. He had the notion that beneath the funereal apparel the woman was elegant and graceful; he could imagine her dressed for a ball. He remembered Italy, Naples, rattled off under his breath the names of a few operas from that time, the good and the bad. Less agreeably, he recalled a notorious evening hosted by the Duke of Richmond at which lascivious details of the Italian episode of the Duke's grand tour when a young man . . .

A youth, considered Handel. I was one, once. Women came and went, there were those of whom the public knew a little, and those others of whom the public knew nothing. A brief interlude with a woman whose face he could not bring to mind; a cantata whose music eluded him. He felt his not very clever heart beat too rapidly, accompanied by the disconcertingly sudden need to sit down. He found a rickety crate and did so. From the Triumphal Arch, a piece of wood the size and weight of a generous roof slate crashed to the floor of the stage amid thunderous oaths and threats from the artificial heavens. Maestro Handel ignored it. What should he do? What did she want? What did she expect? Blackmail was out of the question. Somehow he knew that. But she wanted something.

'I have followed every opera, every performance, every note, as if they were the essence of life itself. I suppose I have been foolish. I know, and I am made constantly aware, that others follow you too.'

'Not so much as they once did, Madam,' Handel muttered to the wood-shavings littering the planking.

'Be that as it may. I am of independent means and can do, travel, think as I wish.'

'I do not doubt it, Madam. But, as you find me . . .'

Handel waved a fattening hand in the chalky noisy air, indicating the theatre, London itself, the very Cosmos, with which he was inextricably involved; he noted with caution the sudden angry edge to her voice. A woman cheated, a woman devoted to redress of a particularly mischievous and lasting kind?

He had nowhere to run and felt too fatigued, suddenly, to care. He longed for an invigorating dish of coffee at Bowes or the Exchange, the pithy smell of ground coffee, the odour of tobacco smoke, the manly darkness, for all the uncomfortable rest. For how many years had this veiled figure spied on his works – virtually the same thing as spying on his person – from the balconies, the stalls? She had clung to him as a succubus: had she brought his aches and pains too?

'Oh, Madam,' he pronounced slowly, hoping she'd be impressed by his deliberateness, 'if you have something to impart to me, do so now. I am not as young as I once was and as gifted in the art of deciphering women's mysteries and caprices. This joke, this visit to me does not find me in best humour, I implore you. You are welcome to have wine with me and talk, if that is what you are come for. If not, if you wish to see yourself as a Dark Woman with secrets which you delight in, I have no business for that. Now, Madam, I have made myself clear. And I have much working to do.'

Bock-bocka-bock went the carpenters, no longer quite so comforting.

Handel wished them all to Hell. He craved communion with his own poor thoughts. Sighing, he looked around him, felt the theatre shape itself awkwardly, ponderously, to the needs of his new music. He was no longer sure, for example, about the prudence of fireworks. He looked up at the cords, ropes and pulleys and planks of the stage-work.

She stayed where she was, slowly becoming part of the set. Yes, he thought, seeing her at the lower part of his vision; I could cast her as a statue and she would be perfect. The thought made him smile.

'You smile, Herr Handel,' she said. 'Some would have it that you never do.'

She stood over him, a faint odour of violets. Really, it was unbearable.

'Mein Gott, this is enough,' said Handel, and, standing, turned his back on her.

For a moment he tensed to receive the sting of a silver blade. It did not come. So. He tapped the tip of his stick off the boards and shuffled back down the gaunt hallway. He acknowledged to himself how frightened he had been of her, how he had denied this to himself as he spoke to her. She had worked to convince him she had known much, a trick, a whim, a nonsense out of her woman's gossipy mind. Or perhaps her brain was sick? He had heard of such things, a distressed woman, fevered of her brain, attaching herself to a composer whose name was on the world's lips, conjuring to herself wild fantasies of romance.

He felt himself fortunate to have made his escape when he did. He felt he had been on the brink of something unpleasant. He stopped, turned, saw her again. He was angry now, impatient. She was standing very still, a black shadow, Pygmalion's statue, looking at him.

Then she lifted her veil. His eyes failed him. At that modest distance he could make out not one single feature, all was a blur. She raised her hand and waved, a single motion in the air, unthreatening, yet solemn. Such an operatic gesture, he thought. But impressive. Doubts tickled him. She was no street walker nor moon-struck withdrawing-room spinster in peril of her nerves. *Have I been, my God, unmannerly, out of fear? I have not acted like any sort of gentleman. If what she said is true, if she really has followed me so devotedly . . .*

Handel raised his stick; the woman turned, as if on cue. Had he frightened her? He recognised something theatrical and staged about it all but was, he admitted to himself, intrigued nonetheless. There was an unwritten aria in all this. She was luring him with her mystery, concocted or otherwise; he could almost hear her accompanying music. He should sing her back to him.

He paused, made to go after her. But she turned and moved away, a woman of bearing, he could see that, slowly absorbed among the stage-builders, singing carpenters, scenery-shifters, agents of make-believe. She moved beyond his vision, into a foggy and unfocussed distance, carrying her enigma with her.

He knew, with a certainty that he had rarely felt about anything, that they could not see her. If he were to question them they would only stare at him blankly; thinking him deranged most of the time anyway.

He knew also that no woman attended her, no coach waited, horses snorting, in the back lanes. *My God,* he mumbled. He felt something roll in his mouth like a furry ball. In the dressing-room which was appointed to serve also as his office and workroom, he poured himself a strong glass of black wine. He quaffed, gulped.

On the floor, on a drawer, on a chair, lay the disrupted and roughly corrected manuscripts. Whoever ushered her into the theatre, they would know. Who was it now who'd told him to expect her? He could not recall. He had been in his workroom, he had been waiting for her. That was all. It was not to be completely understood.

In Venice, he had heard vague tavern-tales of women in masque who were to be seen on midnight bridges, who walked *through walls, who lured men into the watery shadows, never to be seen again. Women who were the spirits of disappointed and tragic loves. No; it was all much simpler than that. This was not Venice with its mists and ghosting marshes. He was overtired, he would recognise his visitor when he gave himself time to think. He gulped again, felt a grateful drowsiness build behind his eyes. Perhaps, in the soft candleglow, he would doze.*

He seated himself comfortably, idled a few pages of the manuscript of Atalanta *through his fingers, pretending to himself that sleep would not, could not intrude on work, and began to doze off. He would sleep and remember the lady, of course he would.*

Bock-bocka-bock sang the hammers, up among the gods and angels. In a moment or two, the pages floated from the composer's fingers.

Thirty-Six

Nos haec novimus esse nihil.

My understanding of Latin negligible, Gay's quotation from Martial, which he used on the title-page of *The Beggar's Opera*, pricked my eyes like grains of salt.

I sat up in bed supping at a luke-warm mug of tea I'd prepared in the deserted kitchen. The book lay in my hands like a revered text. I felt the motion of great unfeeling, invisible wheels.

Swift had visited Belfast – *I dined in the country on most excellent fish* – and tilted his head to view the image of a face on Cave Hill. He had imagined to himself a sleeping giant, gazed up to by alarmed onlookers the size of his thumb. Swift had encouraged Gay to consider a work in which life, in all its tender meanness, might be mirrored and recognised; Italian opera slumbered in its outlandish clothes while around it and over it scuttled unsung the everyday, the real, which was no myth. A new kind of musical entertainment had been produced and new tastes created, or old ones revived. Things had their links, their shifts, their points of meeting.

Handel never did learn the identity of his mysterious visitor; and she had come as he had prepared his opera *Atalanta* for Covent Garden. I felt propelled into the same current of disbelief and mystery. I procured coincidences and invented possibilities. Discovering or creating them filled me with a sensation of energy and excitement. I felt a filtering through of new light. I sipped and read, intoxicated by what I could create between the descriptions of what really happened.

For Handel, for Gay, for Swift, I could invent new lives, new adventures. I could re-invent their world for them, place them in it just as I would place toy soldiers on a make-believe battlefield when I was a child. Now these characters were my toy soldiers, became fictions restless under the pulse of my imagination. I could do whatever I wanted with them, within reason. But reason had very little part in it. Creativity meant contradiction. I wanted to tell everybody. I wanted to tell everybody just the kind of writer I was going to be.

I left the enclosing silence of the house in the careful hands of clocks. On the road, cattle had passed, leaving their hot, dark green mounds of shit. On a twisty tree trunk, a rusting metal sign, declaring *Repenteth, for The Lord Cometh Nigh in Judgement.* The words bled rust. There was the smell of the cattle, their shit, and other smells of raw fields and the sea. I felt light-headed, at ease with myself for the first time in days. I could feel the sodden weight of a slower season press down on me through the quivering diluted sunlight. I rolled up my pullover sleeves and whistled to scare away devils of gloom.

I turned a corner and virtually walked into them, a small patrol of four soldiers, two walking forward, two behind them walking backwards, eyeing the fields, the road and then me.

They carried long-barrelled black guns and one had a radio on his back, the whip-like antenna waving like a conductor's baton to the rhythm of his walk. Their faces were blackened under the eyes. The helmets came down low over their foreheads and their polished black boots crunched loudly on the loose road surface.

They looked me up and down, watched as I crossed out of their path to the far side of the road. A silence, like a shock, enclosed us. They were unbearably young, not like the tough veterans of my war comics with rock-hard, steel-sharp chins and eyes glowing with righteous malice. At least two of them were not as tall as me, and they walked apologetically, side-on to me and suddenly the others laughed. I couldn't make it out. I kept walking, afraid of them, not because they threatened me or were about to, but because they were overpoweringly *there*. They had emerged out of nothing from that apocalyptic world trumpeted by the blast at May's pub. For them to be here, someone had died.

I heard, behind me, the dull mashing noise of their boots receding into the distance: when I looked around they were gone – the road as empty as if they had never been.

I walked on. Here and there I spotted things lying on the road, cigarette-packets, odd shapes of bottles, that I would have carted home to my room, but I was not on my way home.

I had become quite the little magpie: already my room was adorned – or littered – with seashells, predictably enough, my piece of 'Cygnus' jar, an old Ulster Transport Authority bus-stop sign, round and rusted like a harvest moon, and ancient sepia-tone photographs of one kind or another, found in fields, on the road, under rocks. Now and then they reminded me that Atalanta had taken a photograph of me in a wig. Among garbled motives, I began to allow that recollection to fester spicily into the action of making my way back to her place. I imagined I had grown braver, stronger, in the time it took to drain my mug of tea. The sun meant something to me again, even with its noticeable decline in warmth and vigour. I was no longer quite so afraid of meeting Atalanta again and, more importantly, imagined I would be less afraid of myself in her presence. I knew who I was.

Round another corner of the road came Agnes in a car

driven by her father, stern-face, crouched low over the steering-wheel like an angry rat.

But a funny thing happened. Agnes waved to me. A slight, almost apologetic wave, and there was a broken smile to go with it. The car drove away, following the soldiers, and Agnes turned her head and tried to look back. A pleading kind of wave and smile; why? As if she were trying to convey something to me – would we always be friends, even as she wheeled Smithy's little brat around the place? Would I pat it on the head, for her sake? What magic she had drained from me! What sacrifices, and what torments! *Donna Agnes!*

Above the trees, over a field pocked with sheep, a solid *chug-chuga-chug* that seemed to shift in intensity; modulating into a *thock-thocka-thock* sound, diminishing, growing, straight up in the air.

I looked up, trying to pinpoint the sound. I stared into a blue sky which shuffled white clouds about like blank cards; the sun would glide behind a cloud and a dark cool shadow would crawl over the road and slither over the fields.

Then, out of the trees and very high up, the size of a gnat, a midgy, a fragile water-reed thing, I saw the helicopter. It hovered, *thock-thocked*, swung around, its beat becoming a growl, edged over below a cloud, danced back again into the sun with glints of silvery light breaking over it, *thock-thock-thuddy-thuddy-thud.*

What did it look for? An insect, a great Queen guarding its children, keeping an eye on them as they prowled from hedge to hedge. Helicopters in Belfast were common enough; this one over the Ardreagh fields was a foreign thing, out of place where only heron and migrating duck winged about. I stared up at it, shielding my eyes, and felt that it stared back at me, photographed me, processed me, developed me, pinned me to a board. I did not feel secure under its noisy quarrelsome gaze. Like a visiting angel, its presence diminished me.

And then it seemed to roar, send its engine noise down on to the very earth itself and under the earth in some Biblical clamour announcing God only knew what wonders.

I felt the vibrations of the engine, the rattle of its parts. I felt alone, isolated and vulnerable, as if things were abroad that had the power to lift me then and there from the face of the earth and cause me to disappear, imprison me in some dark and alien place where my voice would be stilled and my face obliterated from the memory of the world.

I stared, terrified now, at the helicopter and wondered, marvelled like some medieval alchemist at the melting of metals, how such a tiny thing so high up could send tremors through the earth. And just in time I tore my eyes from the helicopter and looked a dozen yards up the road and saw the massive green-painted bulk of the armoured personnel-carrier – I thanked my war comics for this knowledge of war and armour and death – slowly grinding its way towards me, antennae whipping, wheels huge and eating the tarmac, unstoppable, rude, angry-faced, locked tight within itself like a ferocious shelled animal. I stood there, certain that whoever drove it saw me and didn't care, that he or they and I played out some brief game of *I-dare-you* in the middle of the road.

I jumped to one side and it groaned past me, its observation window winking. The back doors were open and two soldiers dangled their legs over the ends of benches inside. Their laughter was not malicious. They were young. It was a game. One of them waved – as Agnes had waved, and with the same idle inability to communicate. The great engines hammered the personnel-carrier past me with a slow meaningful solidness of movement avalanching rocks might contain. The vehicle grew, enlarged itself under the lens of my apprehension and bewilderment. The resulting image was of something vast and green and overpowering trundling through the world with two laughing teenage soldiers, oblivious to the harnassed terror they sat upon, riding on its back. The soldiers and the machine contradicted each other; I turned and ran and heard the laughter rise and kept going, no longer able to condone such opposites: an alchemist for whom the experiment had gone wrong, and who wanted to erase its consequences from his mind.

I was out of breath. The sun was running along politely into the early afternoon. I sweated. I did not realise or care how far from my own place I'd come. Time seemed to have been measured only in the passing of soldiers, the helicopter's appearance over the trees and the advance of the personnel-carrier. It sounds naive to say I did not know where I was; I knew, when I caught my breath. I knew fair enough. It sounds facile to say that I had not at first intended, at least not directly, to go there.

But I think both notions are true. I found myself there without intending it and once there, was quite conscious of my choices; go or stay. The world seemed full of alien beings and things I could neither manipulate nor understand. I resented their invasion. At the same time, I sensed that it would uproot important things and implant others, that a season of patient learning was upon me. My enthusiasm and elation of earlier in the day had given way to a dull ache of pessimism. I hadn't given my permission for the world to change. The characters in my story were out of control.

When I had turned eighteen my father, embarrassed no doubt by the whole business of birthdays and their implied affections, had given me an envelope with twenty pounds in it. He had turned away, saying he didn't know what I'd like, so here was the money and don't spend it foolishly.

It was a good deal of money. Despite myself, my private dreams, wants, desires, I'd put the money in a Post Office savings bank. I'd been given a savings book, had not put one penny in it since, and had forgotten all about it. Facing the turrets, the absurd elephants, I remembered all about the money, the savings account, the savings book. There was no link between Reginald McKinley's inner gates and my twenty quid. It all just came to me, a set of images, as if some door or gate had been unlocked.

To think of the twenty quid filled me suddenly with sadness. It was pity for my father. The notes had looked limp and pathetic in their frail brown manila envelope. Useless, pleading: perhaps I'd tucked them away for their own protection in the savings account.

The silence of the elephants made me sad. They seemed to symbolise all that had been rendered silent and dumb in the world. They were neither fearsome nor forbidding; they were caricatures, trained performers in some fantastical circus. They were what happened when hired sculptors tried to resurrect memory and dream together in one image.

The twenty quid was what happened when fathers tried to resurrect love from despair and misery. I swallowed the sadness down. I don't know how long I stood before the McKinley elephants and their turrets. I knew that my father was dying in tandem with my mother, but it would take him longer, be more complicated. His world was changing, as my own was, out of his ken; he handed twenty quid to an eighteen-year-old young man who, twenty-four hours ago, had been a seventeen-year-old boy he could order about and organise into his life. I was his symbol of both change and decay.

A wind blew in the trees – it always does at times like these – shaking them. A few anxious leaves flew past and vanished into the hedgerows. I walked under the blind eyes of the elephants and saw the house close before me as I'd seen it for the very first time: the sun touched up bits of bright colour on its ivy and vines, the windows blinked lazily. Again, my instinct was to listen for dogs that never threatened. One cat, possibly two, eyed me from thick clumps of thicket and hedge. I remembered the pathetic cemetery. Birds wailed and called, out of sight. But the house was silent. No music. No sign of Atalanta. It had withdrawn into itself. It was sleeping. Even the blinking of the windows was a kind of nervous but unconscious reflex.

For some odd reason I did not want to enter by the front door. I knew, somehow, that it would be open and the thought of finding it open scared me.

I went round the back of the house. There was the lake, shining peacefully like a contented mirror. Along its edge, the captive tide played childishly in the reeds. A rowing boat lay beached on the grass. I walked over to it. A plastic bag full of letters, photographs, and stones. Atalanta had been out on the lake. Sinking things forever under its glassy silence. God only knew what else she'd got rid of. I thought of my own photograph. I looked back up at the house. From an upstairs window, a faint yellowish glow flickered and quivered. I went round to the front door, and sure enough, it was open.

The hall shimmered in a cold dusty silver light, as if moonlight had accumulated here and become trapped. The faces at the end of the stairs looked at me but did not hint at anything. The doors leading off the hallway were silent too, daring me to open them. I went into the sitting-room where I'd first sat with Atalanta and heard her tale of her mother for whom men killed themselves. The famous opera star.

I had not noticed from the back of the house that the big windows were open, or perhaps I'd have come in that way. In any case the room was exceptionally cold and empty-looking, despite furniture, pictures, piano, the ancient gramophone with a record on it: predictably, something by Handel, *Concerto Grosso in B Minor, Op.6.*

The needle turned and clicked and scraped hopelessly, and I lifted it off. It was slowing down anyway, as if time were putting a finger on it. An utter silence now fell over the room, the agitated metronomic clicking stilled. Photographs lay everywhere, on the couch, big deep chairs, the thick carpet. Faces smiling and solemn; inside and outside shots, shy people, proud people, men, women and children, domestic animals, set against palm-trees, train-stations, old-fashioned cars, wooden-plank houses, deserted streets, crowded avenues, seated at tables, scampering on cropped lawns – unfilled glasses with long precious stems shook in the fingers of firm-mouthed young men in soldiers' uniforms, and fragile looking girls in mushroom hats wide-eyed the camera from the rails of a ship at sea. On the backs of the photographs, cryptic messages, signs, signals, promises, descriptions: *Love, Jo – '45; Me and*

Mags at Jessie's place – July '30; On the 'Titania', near Malta – Summer '38; Ready for Old Adolf (I'm the one in the tights!!!) – Egypt, Cairo, 1943; Maura, agd. 4yrs; 'Les Girls' – Tottenham, July '51; Jo and Wickie and King Lear (Margarie this year!!!); Bandra, Malaya, 1937; Reg. gets a new car – Hollywood, '44; Fitzy and Walter and Cannes (again) – July '66; Me and Marie and Tammy, Mont Saint-Jacques, September '65.

There she was, Marie Atalanta Valle-Dumarc. And Reginald McKinley, smiling, one arm around her shoulder, the other supporting a cat. The same one he had strangled in front of her face?

I looked deep into Reginald McKinley's eyes, through his veneer of a smile. What I saw there was the silence and darkness of a disused well. At the bottom of that well, out of the light, swam sinister cruelties, effigies of emotions, unkindnesses bottled up, tossed down deep into the water in the hope that no one would retrieve them.

I saw in a flash a soft-lights procession of all the other faces in the photographs: spoiled, introverted, champagne and wine, mailing their smiles from distant places, no worries in the world, and, consequently, out of touch with it. They bought new cars, visited the Riviera, made boat trips, played silly imitations of Shakespeare – hadn't I at least attempted *that?* – while dripping with sweat in foreign places in jaunty wars and held cats up by the neck and strangled them. There was a scream echoing and re-echoing from one photograph to another. Even the children in the photographs were held together by bits of wire and string, prepared to perform for the camera, adopt any pose, puppet-like and well rehearsed.

The older the photographs the more deeply-etched the fantasy of normality seemed to be. There was something un-human about the faces, the uniforms, the wars they'd been in; behind the faces you might have expected to see other faces emerging, as masks crumbled and fell away through time.

Originating in this house, or attached to it by invisible lines no distance could break, they had ruled simple and generally honest people whose lives had followed the ritual circlings of the seasons and the moon's grip on the tides and who kept themselves neat, isolated, and God-fearing: while at the same time unknowingly financing the purchasing of fast cars, the Riviera trips, the daft play-acting, the sadistic demise of pet cats. The McKinleys had fallen back into a history they had created for themselves: they were mute lords and masters and mistresses of nothing now but empty rooms and the scratchy needles of ancient record-players. They were entombed forever in their photographs. Dead, surely.

I retreated from the photographs. Books too lay here and there, scattered as if in an attempt to find something hidden away in their pages. Old, leather-bound books, ancient brown pages: littered like the broken wings of birds, all over the floor.

A copy of Ovid's *Metamorphosis* lay broken-backed on one of the fat armchairs, pages torn out by terrible handfuls as if they'd been clumps of hair; Thomas Carlyle – the pages of an essay on Cagliostro, the delightful trickster Beppo Balsamo, lay strewn over the carpet like pieces in a jigsaw puzzle; Robert L. Stevenson's *Kidnapped*; a copy of the Bible; an Encyclopaedia of British Garden Flowers; a compendium of Shakespeare's Sonnets; more Classical writers, Aristophanes, Virgil, Xenophon, Caesar; little books, big books, black books, red books, brown books – tossed and ripped apart as if in a fit of grotesque fury at the very languages themselves.

But the book of Ovid, ripped apart so violently that the knitting of the spine showed, torn and fractured threads steeped in their ancient glue, lay in a spectacular pool of its own destruction, illuminated among the others by the light of its unquiet death. Every single page had been removed with great violence and care. A surgeon's hand had worked over its parchment corpse.

Burnt-out candles stood or lay in their beds of melted wax, all around the room, more or less where they had been placed on the evening of my bizarre charade with Atalanta. The very faint odour of wax burning clung to the air as if afraid to let go. Here and there too, a few old records, mostly Handel and some others, Bach (perhaps Reginald McKinley had liked him, they'd played him at his funeral), Locatelli, Rameau, Corelli and Hadyn. There was no order on anything; the destruction had been abrupt, hasty. Catastrophe had been decided upon and executed without a moment's hesitation or reflection. Everything had fallen under a flailing hand. The candles alone had maintained their dignity and stayed untouched, inviolate.

Now, pathetically, I bumped my foot against some of the tea-cups with their hunt-and-chase sequences painted on them: handles had come off, great V-shaped chips had appeared in the rims. There was the uncomfortable feeling of an entire universe disolving here. I left the room, hearing the curtains brush against the open windows, hearing some kind of voice in their movement. As if a child, hidden somewhere in the photographs, had begun to whimper and sob.

Thirty-Seven

The entrance-hall bore an enormous weight of old time and silence, as if a teacher in a dark corner whispered a history lesson to invisible pupils.

The faces at the bottom of the stairway glowed faintly in the grey light; shafts of watery sunlight protruded through the thin glass on either side of the front door, which I had closed over.

The staircase itself seemed to hum quietly to itself, going upwards into the dark tapestry like a narrow path up the side of a mountain. The girl continued to lead her unicorn in strange and timeless fields. The doors off the entrance-hall were closed and cryptic, eyes with their lids down. I felt that an eternity was flashing by the closed front door; when I went out again, I would step into another time. I climbed the staircase, drawn upwards, feeling unreal and insubstantial.

A quick rogue breeze rattled the edges of windows somewhere else in the house; the odour of melting candle grease was everywhere, like some kind of Romanish incense. At the top of the staircase I looked quickly but deeply into the tapestry; from behind a threaded tree something moved, shifted at the edge of my vision. But it was only a breeze making its way behind the tapestry and along the walls, shaping the contours of the woven picture, giving life and movement to its trapped inhabitants. The unicorn pranced, the girl smiled. The grasses and trees swayed, everything was waiting.

I stood at the top of the staircase, turned, and looked back down into the hallway. A cat padded lightly across the foot of the stairs, stopped, one paw raised in mid-air, stared up at me, hurried on. It left behind the silence, dust-motes hanging in the weak sunlight, the whisper of drafts of air. I felt the burden of my alone-ness. I felt it on my shoulders and on the backs of my legs, a physical sensation as if someone was pushing down and against me. How had Atalanta hoped to survive here, in this abandoned place? The odour of candle grease was thick and sickening now.

I followed it like an animal following the scent of another animal. All the time, I knew where I was going. I'd known *that* from the moment I'd encountered the distraught, silent, empty sitting-room in which – I'd also known – Atalanta had made a final vain despairing attempt to find herself, root herself out from the photographs, the books. Somewhere among them all her name declaimed itself; in the world, it had rebounded upon silence. A yellowish light shimmered on the carpet of the corridor: the door to Atalanta's bedroom was half-open, a shaft, a triangle of candlelight lay on the floor.

I had no fear, just a growing curiosity tinged with a faint anguish. I knew that pushing open the door would be one of the concluding acts in my relationship with Atalanta and the house. There was the sad pull of things going away into irretrievable distances, ships, trains, and buses pulling away from rain-washed quaysides and stations, a hand raised here and there, its action lost and defiant. I felt it all grip the pit of my stomach as I heard the door creak under the weight of my hand.

The room was washed in yellow thick candlelight from half-burned white candles, ones as long as those she'd used downstairs. They were stuck in empty bottles or propped up in their own wax, all over the room, along one side of the bed. The heat in the room was heavy and airless and the window was shut.

On the floor, more photographs, some of them very old, sepia-toned, here and there a tin plate rattled under my feet. Books, too, as old and well-bound as the ones downstairs and just as hastily and thoroughly devastated, torn up, ripped asunder; books, for some reason known only to herself, had become her enemies. As if the weight of their fictions was too much for her, they had conspired in their snug jealous shelves to fool her and suddenly, too late, she had found them out in the lie. Perhaps they had provided her with something, reality of a sort. Then she had seen through them.

Or perhaps she lived in them, had been made by them – a child delving into books for some sort of order, order that the child could not find in the real world of everyday. They had been a means to escape the chaos of her world – I did not know. I saw the destroyed books lying around my feet and they sent out abrupt signals, barely decipherable, jumbled. They were clues; everything was a clue. Atalanta herself was a clue.

She lay on the bed, bathed in the warmth of the candlelight, dressed neatly in what I took to be her wedding-dress, white, preserved, inviolate.

A light veil covered the top half of her face and her mouth was open just enough to show the stained upper teeth. Her feet were together, one hand lay stiffly at her side and the other hung out sharply at a ninety-degree angle to her body, a theatrical, dramatic gesture. Just as dramatic and rehearsed were the tiny white tablets sprayed over the carpet and one or two of the violated books. A bottle, dark brown glass, lay upturned just under the bed. She had been drinking wine, a bottle half-empty stood with righteous stiffness on the floor beside the bed, there was no glass.

I could visualise her with the bottle to her lips, alone, hearing the silence of the house, the lake, the fields finally overtake her. For how long had she ferried papers, books, photographs out into the middle of the lake, watched them sink or float or glide away on secret currents, out of her sight?

At what point had she known it was hopeless, too much, had sat down, already drunk, to decide upon a suitable finale? The world did not watch, no one did.

And I had gone, disappeared, retreated, safe behind my own walls. Her only spectator, witness, audience, call it what you will – how many roles had I played in Atalanta's searching eyes? Reginald had left her an inheritance of silence and photographs. Some of them proclaimed an acceptable past; some, the brutal indecency of it all. In which photographs had she been Marie, in which Atalanta?

She had dressed herself as she had wanted to be remembered: white, virginal, celebratory. She had stretched out on the bed, having tidied it first, feet close together, head back, the bottle of tablets in her hand, the wine waiting to wash the tablets down. Sleep, a final need to sleep. A gathering exhaustion, a feeling of having worked in vain, a great deal of energy wasted. Above all, the desire not to think, to silence the tickings of mind and memory.

I knew she was dead. I stared into her face, into the half-open eye-lids, into the unseeing pupils. I put my ear to her breast and heard nothing, not a tremble, a murmur of life. A sweet odour lingered around her mouth. Her face was white, a bluish tinge under the eyes. Tiny white sewn flowers sat grouped together by circles of thread in her hair.

Suddenly I was aware of the camera, of the photograph she'd taken. Panic thrilled me into a need for action, movement. I began searching, snuffing out one or two candles as I blundered about the room. At one point I opened the window and a breeze silenced some more candles. The room cooled, it became easier to breathe. I searched under the bed, a jungle of fluff and dust and dead human hair. I searched everywhere I could think of and shuffled through the wrecked books and dilapidated photographs. An unnatural tranquillity, a tortured peace, had settled over everything.

At last I found the camera on top of a dusty sideboard. There was still film in it and I could only assume that it was the same roll of film that had been in it on the day of our masquerade. I sincerely hoped it was. Any pathos that had crowded around me as I looked down at Atalanta's body dissolved in my panic to find the camera and the film; I opened the camera, pulled out the film, let the light destroy it, blind it forever. I tossed the roll of film on to the floor, then was overcome by a sense of terror that somehow, by some technical or chemical miracle or other, the images on the paper might still be developed. I stuffed the roll of film into a pocket. The opened camera too seemed to still contain decipherable secrets and revelations: I held it in my hand as if it might run away. While catching the camera I noticed the thin sheet of paper under the wine bottle: '*Honour me.*'

The two words seemed to shout out of the lined, childish page, words from another age. They had been written, scrawled – the handwriting was all over the place – for the world, or me alone, for all I knew, to find. Left, ironically, beneath a wine bottle. I stifled a sudden nervous giggle. My hands were starting to shake and I had not given in to or acknowledged my nervousness. Suddenly it began to seep through my pores. I was sweating. *Honour me.* Of course. In what way? Was it up to me? There was no one else around. No one else would understand the call of this obligation. Atalanta would be open to prying, speculative eyes, her life – that which was portrayed in the photographs – would be revealed to the sniggering world. Honour me. *Protect me.* Close my life over, keep it secure from the world. But was it up to *me*? Of course it was. There was no one else, no evidence of anyone else; no need for anyone else.

I went out to the top of the staircase and into the blessed half-light. I sat down on the top stair, looking down into the hallway. In one hand I held the opened camera; in the other, Atalanta's last words on the subject of her life. In between, sat the irony that was me.

Thirty-Eight

I do not know how long I sat at the top of the stairs.

The entire house began to tremble, moan and shake. A heavy snarling sound, loud and vicious, seemed to descend upon the roof: I recognised above the hard gritty roar of helicopter engines. The tapestry behind me swayed and protested; the little unicorn pranced, the girl twisted her body in a jerky spasmodic dance. The noise seemed to pour over the house like a waterfall, down the walls, over the roof. The big front door rattled slightly; windows reverberated and hummed. I stood up. I looked up at the ceiling as if I might be able to look through it. The helicopter lifted, the noise decreased. It moved away and a shaken and anxious silence swept the house again.

I shoved Atalanta's note inside the open body of the camera. I thought of what I was about to do and tried to find a way out of it. There was none. The note, written in the knowledge that I would, some day, come back, had sealed the affair.

I went downstairs, dumped the camera, roll of film, note, in the boat, went in, scoured downstairs and in her bedroom until

I had managed to collect as many photographs, recent and old, including those which displayed Atalanta so cruelly, as I could. I worked for a long time, the light receding along the lawns, over the lake. Afraid to turn on the house lights, I worked occasionally by candlelight. I felt absolutely no fear, just a ragged-ended sense of duty and appropriateness.

One by one I ferried cartons, plastic bags and small boxes out to the boat. Birds sang discreetly in the black trees, the sun slipped down with no sound, the world was coming to an end without a murmur of protest. Now and then I forced myself to sit for a moment, get my breath back. And I'd search around in the house for an unopened bottle of wine; eventually I found one, opened it, drank deeply.

The alcohol sped through my bloodstream like hot oil. I was doing everything now against the rules of the world I'd lived beyond this house. I was forging a new world, with new rules. I felt strong, unassailable. I moved from room to room with gathering momentum, a force contained within the walls of the house, held there like some perverse and dangerous result of a physics experiment which might threaten the stability of the world if it were unleashed. The house was warm and the breeze in the open air cool, so that I sweated and dried off by turns. The books I ignored. They were cyphers I could not bother to unravel. Their secrets belonged to Atalanta. The final task was physically the most difficult. I sat in the shattered sitting-room and finished off the wine. I was drunk, but clear-headed. Physical activity seemed to have used up whatever energy was in the booze and at the same time diluted its sedative effect.

Atalanta's body looked flimsy and insubstantial as it lay in its pure immaculate white on the bed. However, I could not lift her. The thought that I might have to submit her to one final indignity filled me with anger. Was anger a form of love? It was the energy of sheer brutal anger that enabled me to cocoon the body in the top-cover of the bed, anger that permitted me to drag Atalanta on to the floor: anger still, intense and blood-tasting in my mouth, which enabled me to drag her body down the hall, down the stairs, through the sitting-room, over the grass and on to the boat.

I pushed the boat into the water and steadied it. Night birds skimmed the surface of the lake. A cushion rested her head. I went back several times to the sitting-room and the bedroom. I collected as many candles as I could and lined the boat with them. I gathered up the tablets spilling out of the little brown glass bottle. They too went on board. The wine bottle I didn't worry about. I flattened out the sheets and blankets on the bed so that no imprint of Atalanta's body remained there. I made one stop in the kitchen and found what I was looking for after a few minutes. I carried the rusty tins of paraffin – the kind of tins kids used for cricket-stumps along the roads – and bottles of paint-thinners up to the boat and sprinkled, then poured their contents all over Atalanta, the candles, the photographs, everywhere.

In the sitting-room, a few candles glittered and spat, tossing odd shadows here and there, patient light. Now I was filled with intolerable sadness, as if a well had been suddenly tapped within me, a well dammed up for too long.

I sat on the edge of the couch and wept openly, loudly, drunkenly. Tears thickened my mouth, saliva and tears ran through my fingers. Here was all the sadness and despair of the world, concentrated, in this room, in the candlelit darkness, in the boat bobbing at the edge of the shore. I wept for the final lonely days of my mother, my father's blind and stubborn loneliness which was caressed by regrets he had never had time – given himself time – to voice; for Atalanta McKinley, whom I had loved in some reckless and uninformed fashion, unaware of anything she felt or needed, for only in masquerade had she found any voice and that voice had been distorted and untrue. Oddly, I wept for Agnes and for Smithy. I wept for the kind of loneliness they had brought into the world. Totems of sorrow and abandonment passed me by in that hot dark room. I saw Johnny Henderson's face on that day he'd handed me the card from Atalanta. I saw also the destroyed face of the girl the fishing-boat had brought in. The world seemed to live in the eyes of these people. They had known, even for one obliterating second, all that was to be known. As Johnny Henderson threw his double-twelve and the world disintegrated around him, other worlds had also disintegrated at that very instant; worlds which could not be rebuilt. Nothing, in the end, escaped.

I stood up, emptied, feeling a sense of relief. Calmly, all fuss and panic gone from me, as if I moved under water, I looked about the room for things I might have overlooked, things not done, acts not completed. I found everything in order, more or less. In charge of Atalanta's funeral rites, her appointed High Priest, I inspected her relinquished temple with a cold, surgical eye. The piano sat mute and closed with nothing left to play; decanters of spirits, taken out of their designated closets, flickered and blinked with points of candlelight, the golden and bronze liquids unmoving, still as solids. Roses and other flowers had died and faded here, their perfumes no longer discernible in the hot waxy air. I closed my eyes: I could still hear her voice, the good and open voice of the little girl – Marie? – who had taken me to the beach.

In the kitchen I'd found a large box of matches. I stared at the remaining candles, at their sword-shaped blades of light, then went back down to the boat.

Thirty-Nine

Blind.

To be blind. To exist in darkness, to be in a place where there could be no light. To move with that darkness contained in the eyes to the end of one's days. To have relied so much on the light, then to see it fade, then withdraw altogether. Samuel Sharp, Guy's Hospital surgeon, friend, lecturer, had done his best. The blindness was relentless, a familiar inevitable thing.

And still it was mouthed in the coffee-houses and theatres that he had, in his Jephtha, produced the greatest of all oratorios. While rowing against the dark. He had been prepared to lose the light but not, somehow, quite so quickly, so finally. There had been days, weeks of continued writing, holding back the closing curtains, having more to say, not wanting to leave the half-lit stage.

Then there had been that sad and omen-laden business with the child of Thomas Linley, a musician who had performed his work at Bath. Linley had named his first-born son George Frederick – the child had died in infancy. A man can find himself surrounded by only so many omens. A man must, in the end, submit. For those who wished to know, for any who would take time to understand

and appreciate it, that was what he had written throughout his Jephtha: *How dark, O Lord, are Thy decrees.*

Well a man might ask! But the Almighty did not answer from fiery bushes in these days; the age of miracles was over. Angels moved through the oratorio like promises. There had to be more. There had been too much of life to have it snuffed out like a wax candle; darkened, and then snuffed out. Fame had come, dwindled, come again; in its second coming darkness had covered the world.

There was something amiss with the run of his life. His energies seemed scattered, dispersed. Now and then friends helped him in and out of their parlours, it was as if he could hear above their pity the soft moan of regret. If there was a God, and he had written that there was, then presumably this sound came from Him. Was it too much to ask? Another year, two, of light? So that the faces of his friends would shine again, the light on a glass open the doors of happy evenings? So that the music would move more lightly under his pen?

There were those who jotted and scored for him; it was not, never could be, the same thing. In the consuming dark, fears grew and lurked like hideous toadstools. He had begun to feel that Sharp avoided him: worst of all was the feeling that friends saw you, knew you could not see them, and passed you by, the patience at your blindness, your patent disability, an embarrassment to them. At night, unable to distinguish night from day, he would raise himself up in his bed and call out. Did someone hide beyond his eyelids? Did some old enemy, or some friend? Did a watcher take up position at the foot of his bed and stare at him as he slept – even as he sat up, frightened, and listened?

Now and then in dreams he saw perfectly well. He saw again the faces of women who had enticed and won him, and whom he had won. Their mystery and eternal passion had once flattered him. He had belonged to them and had thrown his music at the rest of the world as widely as youth would permit, not caring for fame, understanding, sympathy, love – except from them. They had been puzzles he had set out to solve. He had both succeeded and failed. He had worn the subsequent bachelorhood well, with dignity; he'd known other men to go to drink.

Loneliness, the certain emptiness which the loss of a loved woman caused, had suddenly destroyed both good music and good men.

Then pity had flowed like sour vinegar. It could quench no thirst. Good men, their music decent and listenable, showing all the promise of better things, ruined because of pity. He would have none of it. No pity! And he would allow himself none. Not in the past. Not because of things in the past. Not because of the present or the dark future.

Pen and ink. He wrote, feeling the paper with one hand, fingering it into place, a fumbler – no pity, mind! – but determined. He would give a party. He would invite his friends, and they could invite whom they liked. Wine, decent meat. Some would bring their instruments and there would be music. The smell of tobacco. A man's company.

He made out a list of names. He drew up another of wines; port, some French stuff. There were those who muttered – God! He could not see them – that he had succumbed, like the others, to secret drinking. They could put about what they liked. He knew his own strengths. Madeira. And some rum, maybe two bottles. Alas, he could no longer indulge in his fancy of decanting, someone would have to do that for him.

So! Just as there were those who quipped that his jovial gods did not extend as far as just above the mechanical clouds! That they were too lumpen, fat, robust! They loved the earth too much! Ha! That now, could very well be true. What of it? Wine came from the earth, not from the clouds. Teufel! Scribble-scribble.

Names, lists, more names. He had not had a bath or a decent wash in a very long time and a long rough shift covered him from shoulders to toe. He was bald, hopelessly so, and there was no way he could tell what wigs looked best and which looked worst these days. Most of the time it was easier not to bother with one.

There was, however, the tedious business of dressing. He concluded his lists. He would dictate the invitations. He found – more fumbling, groping about – his stick and hammered on the floor. The sound shook him, the room itself seemed to shake too. He hammered again. Now the sound seemed to reverberate through the house. The house became a kind of drum. He hammered again, again, again. No answering step on the landing. No word. Nothing. He listened. The sound of a carriage on the street below. Nothing more. Nothing.

He was seized by childish fears, unreasonable panic. Things in jars in locked rooms. *He stood up from the table. He felt his list, the pen, the ink, fall away into a deep-soundless well. He had to find the door. He dropped his stick, clatter-clatter. Dark.* Alchemy of fire and flesh. *He heard the deep throbbing protest of his heart. He fell, felt himself falling, the world turning on its axis independent of his angle to it, or something very odd happening. He came down with a dull awkward thud against the side of his unmade bed. He sat there, listening. Nothing. He was alone. No one came, no sound, no voice at all in the house, or in the entire world.*

This silence was God. He sat on the floor, crumpled like a fat child, and wept.

Forty

Rain. Above the gantries the sky was the colour of melting lead. Iron and steelplate bled into the gutters in steady, noisy torrents. The smell of iron and rust and acetylene lay everywhere like a blanket of mist over a field. The taste of iron sat in the mouth like the taste of blood. No braces now, still I had metal and iron on my tongue all the time.

Now and then I had the idea that I was breathing iron on the air. The noise of men shouting, of machines groaning and steel things rubbing against each other was everywhere, an unstoppable clamour as if from the darkness of some unearthly forge. There were places where the noise did not penetrate or did not seem to go: here, I would retreat with a cigarette and a newspaper. There were seconds when a hush fell over everything, as if all the fires and torches had been snuffed out, an incredible catch in the breath. In these moments it was as if time stopped, buckled, went back on itself. Then everything would begin all over again.

The sky sat above the cranes and scaffolding and gantries

like a dirty cloth thrown over everything, the way you'd toss a rag over a pile of dirty dishes, to keep it out of God's sensitive sight. Here and there pools of rust-coloured water spiked up under the rain. Hard-hats bobbed about like coloured corks in a massive bathtub; figures in overalls flitted like delicate priests involved in sacred celebrations from one steel altar to the next. Doors opened and closed again. Metal groaned and gave birth to other sounds, delicate, sweet, like the sound of flutes. Boots with metal toecaps ricocheted off the concrete pathways.

Men whistled to one another, yelled, laughed, munched thick-breaded sandwiches and spooned sugar and tea from little double-decked tins, red and white for tea and sugar, poured milk from thin whiskey-bottles. We moved like ants in tall grass, the iron stems around us always, moving now and then with ponderous slowness, the great slabs of ships growing up slowly out of nothing.

Now and then the sun broke through and shone on everything in patches as it would through the undergrowth of a rain-forest. Goliath strode over all. Great lights appeared in the gantries, men sang: light shivered and coiled like snakes down the steel rails, blinded the eyes in sudden flashes as if angels had sprung up among us and shone the light of their faces upon us.

I sat and munched my aunt's sandwiches, opened my overalls to cool down, hugging my corner of the shed with jealous pride.

Here, from where I ran messages and relayed petty unimportant orders, I had my imagination penned like a frightened animal. I used it in small doses, or perhaps I might say that I took it out for moments at a time and petted it, to get me through the day. I was mortally afraid of everything for a long time. The sky was too high, the feeling of being shut in too extreme and persistent. I was shut in more by having to be there than by any physical thing. I detested having to punch a card, going and coming, being too far away from quiet streets and the rest of humanity to be able to go for a walk at lunchtime. I needed to discuss things with myself. In the lavatory I found a certain relief from mounting nervous tension in the newspaper photographs of half-naked girls. The ensuing guilt and sensation of having been watched by the entire 'Yard became too much. I crowded the energy of this tension and all others back over into my corner.

Here, a photograph sent by Andrew Bell, now ministering with unabated boyish enthusiasm for cricket on some Pacific island where the Welsh had not landed, was tacked determinedly to a wooden beam on the wall. Andrew Bell, in cricket whites, smiled back at the camera and took up a defence position at the wicket. I had the feeling that the anticipated ball had never been bowled.

Behind him, smiling dark-faced figures mocked the soul-robbing mystique of the square machine. Palm-trees waved and bobbed. Sunshine oozed over everything, thick as custard; for minutes at a time I would stare into the photograph until the figures in it began to move. I was writing stories at home in my upstairs room in my aunt's place, tired out after a day's work but fired by other drives. I spent a lot of time creating a story from Andrew Bell's photograph. Pinned also to the beam were my lists, whose lives were as briefly colourful as butterflies.

I had a list of men in the shed who took sugar in their tea and who brought their own, and those who didn't bring their own but took it in their tea also. I had a list of men who took milk – and brought their own – and who didn't bring their own but took it nonetheless. There was a list of men who smoked Woodbines, a list for those who smoked Gallaher's; and these had a sub-list of colours, Blues, Greens, and Reds. Tens and twenties came next. So that when a man shouted for a packet of fags and handed you up money you didn't have to ask him which brand he wanted.

There was a list of what days I would have off in the coming month, sometimes I'd have to work Saturdays. There was a biscuits list and a chocolate sandwich list and even a scone list. These changed rapidly. Lists presented me with order and shaped my day. There was a list of rostered days for when I'd take an early lunch and when a late one. I ran messages all over the place and enjoyed the break from the shed. But the world remained far away, and Napoleon's Face reclined on top of Cave Hill without making so much as a grimace.

When the great hooters sounded I was off home, across the bridges with the other armies of cloth-capped men, our tired murmur creasing the waters of the Lagan. We carried empty lunch-boxes and an air of suppressed power. We dispersed through the wee streets of the city like water being slowly siphoned off some great lake. Our newspapers carried stories of horrors it was hard to comprehend, outstripping what had happened at Ernest May's place by a very long way. On their way to school, children fell over the bodies of men shot in the head, left in gutters. Warnings settled over whole areas of the city like the onset of a plague: the darkness was tainted with suspicion and worry about how to get home safely. Taxi drivers from one side of the city refused to cross the Lagan into another, leaving their passengers to stroll across the silent naked backs of the bridges, heads down, fear in their hearts, like refugees making the last few hundred yards into their homeland. No one ever discussed politics in public places, but made determined and largely successful efforts to create conversations about other things.

On weekends, whenever I stayed in the city, I made the best of it by crawling timidly from one pub to the next until I got to feel safe in them, most of the time drinking some form of lemonade but gradually becoming accustomed to the slow drag of beer.

Here I heard conversations of old cloth-capped men who had fought in various wars, backed unnamed and unprofitable horses, cheered football teams who had not deserved it. Here I watched the young spivs dolled up for the night chatting up the girls and watching themselves in the bar mirrors. A country boy, I imitated their drawl and dress for a while and then gave it up. I bought a pair of corduroy jeans and a couple of buttoned-down collar shirts and kept my hair short. I met a girl and took her to the cinema once or twice and then one evening she didn't turn up outside C&A's where I'd agreed to meet her and that was that. On Saturdays when I wasn't working and had decided not to go home, I browsed contentedly in bookshops, made a few purchases. Eventually I bought a typewriter and taught myself, over many nights, to type. Now my typed stories, corrected, rewritten, were ready to send out to the world.

My aunt made me big breakfasts and hearty dinners, sniffling all the time about the lino-covered table, warned me about staying out late at night, told me to go home to my father as often as I could. The triple security barriers of Royal Avenue fascinated me; their turn-stile football match atmosphere made negotiating them a kind of game. In the evenings the city was split by the occasional sound of a far-away ambulance: once my aunt called me to the door, late at night. Listen, she said; and other doors opened. We listened to the soft liquid smack of gunfire in the distance.

I would take the bus home to Ardreagh and tell myself I was going to visit my mother's grave, change the flowers, see that it hadn't become choked over with weeds. I would get off the bus in the square, listen to the workmen working evenings to resurrect a shiny new pub where Ernest May's old place had been, look around the square for faces that I knew, seeing fewer of them as time passed.

The square would look dismal and rejected under the rain. The Unknown Soldier looked like a caricature of his former arrogant determinism. My father would be waiting in his wee egg van, his hair thinning and his face gaunt, a man wasted by loneliness and an indefinable sense of guilt. The house smelled of dishes not washed, just as a graveyard often became tainted by the graves unvisited. Things lay around, articles of clothing, cigarette butts, newspapers, in no order, neatness defied, everything collapsing upon itself. Here and there, however, a few religious tracts lay like discarded bookie's dockets.

We would sit through interminable hours of trying to converse, become of interest to one another: now and then one of his brothers would join us and the evening would get longer.

I couldn't sleep in my old room anymore. That was all over. My father would see me off to the bus and wave as if he were waving to a stranger. It saddened me, but I could do nothing about it. And of Atalanta, or any connection he might have imagined I'd had with her, he made no mention. She just hadn't been seen around for a very long time, and, with a woman like that – as Mr M'Whinney remarked to me – you could expect anything.

Now and then the bus back to the city was stopped by a roadblock and soldiers or police would board it, tip up the back seats and peer under them, let us proceed. I often fell asleep on the return trip, exhausted, overcome with the effort of just being at home. Gradually, the red city became a place of refuge, the place where, anonymous, I could be myself. Whenever I went back to Ardeagh, I had to become someone else, assume a fake and cumbersome identity for the duration of my visit. The city began, slowly, to give me new life and I began to want more of it, grow eager for it, my trips to the places of my former life becoming less and less frequent. Agnes Fielding and Walter Smith were gone.

Now and then I sat at my place facing the wall in the shed and remembered, with a delicious anguish, the dreamlike vision of the boat in flames, gliding over the lake.

It was a comforting, rather than a frightening recollection. The memory of a duty carried out. In my ears was the sound of men shouting, hammering, drilling, the squeal of steel against steel; and in my eyes the boat drifting on some hidden current, finding its place in the centre of the lake as if guided there by an invisible hand, starting to break apart under the pressure of heat and flame. The sound of wood cracking and burning filtering across the lake, tinged faintly with an odour I'd caught in the air in the desolation of Ernest May's pub the night it was blown up, the smell of flesh burning.

I'd stood on the edge of the lake and waited until a final thick tongue of flame licked upwards and the boat rocked under its burden, then disintegrated. It dissolved into the waters of the lake until there was nothing left to see, and the ripples on the surface of the lake diminished and everything returned to silence and dark.

Round my neck I wore, on a piece of string, a tiny golden apple which had fallen into the bottom of the boat when I'd settled Atalanta on her cushion. I wore it as both symbol and keepsake. I knew already that the memory of my time with her would fade and assume a variety of confusing, indiscriminate colours and tones. Sooner or later it would be as if she had never really existed, had been a creation of my lonely and unsatisfied teenager's mind. The tiny golden apple might suggest a reality to Atalanta and me which no amount of time could diminish or disfigure. And yet, when I purchased map after map of France, delved into travel guide after travel guide and still could not find a place called Mont Saint-Jacques, I was not surprised.

Day passed into day. Night into night. My hands touched oil and grease and metal and smelled of these things constantly, no amount of washing could remove the stench. My visits home became replaced by postcards, hasty letters bearing no real substantial news. Sometimes my father came to the city, we walked around it in a guarded silence. Not once did he mention a football match.

Over tea in my aunt's place I would show him what I'd written recently, the neat typed sheets, virtually daring him to comment, ridicule them, but he did not. He swept his wet eyes over them, grunted graciously, passed them back to me. He couldn't have read them and he found the ritual of pretence tiring. On cue, he would then stand up and say it was time he was off.

Day into day. Every morning giant cranes and gantries rose up around me, shrugged off their thin blankets of gulls; mythic, incredible, lords of a Lilliput of iron and fire.

Coda

Extract of letter from Jonathan Swift to a Dr Elias Camberwell, Minister, of Greenwich, London, dated 1721:

'. . . and I dined in the Country on most excellent Fish. The Country here is most pleasing and you will know my Need to take long Walks. We spoke greatly on the Effeminancy of the Italian Opera and what must be undertak'n to cause an Alteration to it. I was too much alarm'd by the Face I had discern'd on the Mountain above Bellfast Town and spoke of it a long time. Sir, said he, I do not much have Reason to go to Bellfast, but if you have it there is a Face on a Mountain and you seeth a Face, therefore I will take your Word upon it! Surely, then, Sir, you would have us to be small Men indeed! I have a good Digestion and do not Dream, waked or sleeping. We walked by his House and he held it was too modest a thing, that he would build another near Water or he would provide that too. He is most civil in his new Country Manner but abrupt. He maketh me to think that I seeth Faces as I do also turn so disagreeably in my Head at times, and that the First was a product of the Second and of the same Nature. He would hold that Imagination is a Disease, so practical is he become in the Country . . .'